Comments on *Why Are Gas Prices So High?* by William Bezanson

"What Mr. Bezanson is out to change is nothing less than the human psyche itself.
. . . We are launched into an uplifting exploration of how interiorizing change in the psyche first could result in lifestyle changes which can enhance all aspects of our family and social interaction.
. . . I've read many self-help and psychological books. None was better than this book at providing such an ongoing uplift.
. . . *Why Are Gas Prices So High?* should be considered as a possible gift for the naysayer in your family who doesn't want to entertain anything but the traditional technology."
 - Mary-Sue Haliburton, Editor, *Pure Energy Systems Network,* Sept 13, 2006

"The central idea in this book is very, very interesting.. . . . It is a brilliant idea to address environmental issues by bringing to life some real-life characters in a novel."
 - Jawad Gilani, Host, "The Correspondent", *CHUO Radio*, Ottawa, ON (From an interview broadcast April 6, 2006)

"This book is a fictional account of how a lesson in saving gasoline by slowing down your driving speed can lead to other benefits as well. . . . A lesson to slow down and gain more spiritual peace."
 - "Author seeks answers, and gets a lot more", *Nepean This Week*, April 28, 2006, page 12.

Why Are Gas Prices So High?

William Bezanson

Copyright © 2006 William Bezanson

© Copyright 2006 William Bezanson.
All rights reserved. No part of this publication may be reproduced, stored in a retrieval system, or transmitted, in any form or by any means, electronic, mechanical, photocopying, recording, or otherwise, without the written prior permission of the author.

Note for Librarians: A cataloguing record for this book is available from Library and Archives Canada at www.collectionscanada.ca/amicus/index-e.html
ISBN 1-4122-0094-6

Printed on paper with minimum 30% recycled fibre. Trafford's print shop runs on "green energy" from solar, wind and other environmentally-friendly power sources.

Offices in Canada, USA, Ireland and UK
This book was published *on-demand* in cooperation with Trafford Publishing. On-demand publishing is a unique process and service of making a book available for retail sale to the public taking advantage of on-demand manufacturing and Internet marketing. On-demand publishing includes promotions, retail sales, manufacturing, order fulfilment, accounting and collecting royalties on behalf of the author.

Book sales for North America and international:
Trafford Publishing, 6E–2333 Government St.,
Victoria, BC V8T 4P4 CANADA
phone 250 383 6864 (toll-free 1 888 232 4444)
fax 250 383 6804; email to orders@trafford.com

Book sales in Europe:
Trafford Publishing (UK) Limited, 9 Park End Street, 2nd Floor
Oxford, UK OX1 1HH UNITED KINGDOM
phone 44 (0)1865 722 113 (local rate 0845 230 9701)
facsimile 44 (0)1865 722 868; info.uk@trafford.com

Order online at:
trafford.com/05-3106

10 9 8 7 6 5 4 3 2 1

Dedicated To Susan

In Memory of Kathleen (Atwater) Peterson

Acknowledgments: I am grateful to the following people for ideas, reading earlier drafts, feedback, and suggestions: Greg Bezanson, Robert Glosssop, Brian Matthews, Hayley McRae, Arlen Michaels, Sylvia Pollard, Ginny Twomey, Audrey Van Sertima, and Susan Van Sertima. The cover illustration is by Brenda Johima.

Note: Characters in this novel are fictitious. Names assigned to these characters are not meant to represent real people. On the other hand, place names, such as Ottawa and Calgary, represent real places.

By the same author: *Performance Support Solutions: Achieving Business Goals Through Enabling User Performance,* Victoria, BC: Trafford Publishing, 2002

CONTENTS

PROLOGUE: The present time: Seeing Mom off 7

Part A: Three Years Ago

1. Why are gas prices so high? — 15
2. Drive the speed limit — 23
3. Becoming a believer — 29
4. Trying something new — 37
5. The word spreads — 47
6. Backlash — 57

Part B: Two Years Ago

7. Newton's third law — 65
8. Drive the self-limits — 75
9. A life of its own — 93
10. Reactions to the L-movement — 101

Part C: One Year Ago

11. Why drive the speed limit? — 119
12. Creating the future — 131
13. One — 145

Part D: The Present Time

14. A new world — 165

PROLOGUE — *The present time: Seeing Mom off*

"I think I'll buy the books myself," Claire Atwater called out to the others.

Peter was the first to respond. "Are you sure?" he yelled.

The children ignored the exchange. They were used to their parents changing their minds, and shouting out last minute instructions or itinerary changes or news flashes as they were leaving the house. They had their own agendas: wolfing down some cereal while catching a bit of television over their hurried breakfasts.

Why Are Gas Prices So High?

When had the Atwater family never been in a hurry? This seemed like simply the way it was, throwing a sweater on as you ran down the stairs, gulping down orange juice, watching television while propping the phone to an ear to check on the bus schedule. Bumping into parents or sisters or cats in the kitchen. Snatching a quick look at the paper to check on the world. "How was your sleep?" "Fine."

And yet, how ironic!

"How very ironic," thought Jane to herself. Eighteen years old, she had reached an age where she could observe situations such as this and develop a reasoned, critical view. This family, of all the families in the world, she realized, should not be rushed. What a scandal it would cause, if the rag mags caught wind of the turmoil in the household routine of this very family!

Jane was proud of her mother. And her father. And even Mary, her sister, two years younger.

But mostly she was proud of her mother. Wow! How many teenaged girls have a mother who changed the world?

The present time: Seeing Mom off

Yes, of course her mother would buy the books. And she would do this and that and the other thing. All before ten o'clock!

Where was there a bookstore open before ten, for goodness sake? But her mother would find one.

Yes, Claire would buy the books. On her way to give her talk. On her way to or from that service club breakfast. Which one was it this time? Rotary? Lions? Yeah, one of them. And she would drive the speed limit, while doing it all.

After all, wasn't she the "Speed Limit Lady?"

Jane had originally been embarrassed by her mother's quick rise to fame three years ago. People flashing "L" to her and snickering. She felt so mortified ... she only wanted to blend in, not to be different, not to stand out.

That was then. But just this past spring, her Grade 12 Social Studies class had done a study of the movement that her mother had started. Cool! And she had done a special project that was based on the movement.

The good news was that her parents had been sensible enough to coach Jane and Mary through the maturing

9

process while being exposed to the spotlight of the world. The bad news was that it was rough going for a while, with publicity, threats, and notoriety. But they came through it all, as better individuals and a better family.

"Good luck, Mom," Jane whispered, as Claire leaned over to kiss her cheek. "And good knowledge, skill, speaking ability ..." she corrected herself.

"And good performance!" piped up Mary, wanting to be included.

Peter beamed with pride, as he kissed Claire good-bye. Which was he more proud of? His wife, for going to give a breakfast talk to a service club? Or their daughters for having internalized his teaching that it's not luck that's important, but knowledge, skill, performance, inspiration, hard work, and so on?

"So I don't need to get the books?" he asked.

"No, I can easily swing by the store," Claire said. She wanted the books for that evening's dinner party. She and Peter liked giving out books as gifts for their guests.

Yes, the dust would settle a bit once Claire got away.

The present time: Seeing Mom off

Jane called out to her from the front door, "Slow down, Mom. Don't burst the bubble!"

"Thanks, Honey!" What a delight her family was for her! Claire smiled, glowing inwardly. And glowing outwardly. A calm serenity had enveloped her person. Not forced. Not a sham, masking over her household rushing. But a sincere calmness, letting her smell the roses.

Yes, the world had really changed! And she had started it! Well, not really ... She hadn't actually started it. She had simply been there when it started. "Come on, now!" she told herself. "How could one person do all that, especially me?"

Was it knowledge, skill, performance, and all the rest, as Peter would say? Or was it totally luck? Yes, for sure, this time she was lucky.

And perhaps a bit inspired. Yes, luck, and inspiration. Lucky to be inspired. And lucky enough to tell Joe and the others. And lucky that it all went Click!

"And here I am," Claire realized. "Lucky enough to be going off to tell my story to a breakfast meeting of yet another service club! Yet another speech! How many have there been? And panel discussions? And conference presentations?

"How many? Jane will know. She's keeping a scrapbook."

Claire rehearsed her speech in her mind. No notes. She loved talking without notes. She loved the thrill of not knowing what she would say, or in what sequence, or using which examples, or for how long. She loved just telling her story. She loved going into a room, forming her first impression of the audience, and then just going with the flow.

Scary, yes! Living on the edge, for sure! And what a profound thrill, when she pulled it off! Again and again.

"Yes, they must like what I have to say!" thought Claire. "I keep getting invited."

Her hope was that her story would make a profound change in the lives of a few people for each of her audiences or readers, even one or two people.

Yes, telling her story. Spreading the word. That's what she loved to do.

Part A: Three Years Ago

CHAPTER 1 — *Why are gas prices so high?*

"Why are gas prices so high?"

Joe Carboni was moaning, grumbling about his pet peeve.

He was getting fed up, after what seemed like a lifetime of complaining about the rising price of gas for his car. He was ready to do something about it, but he didn't know what.

He decided to bring up the topic with Claire Atwater when they met for lunch later today. "Good old Claire!"

thought Joe. She always had some sensible suggestion for the various problems that Joe had in his life.

It seemed like a normal day, driving to work, stuck in slowly-moving traffic. A blaze of golden colours beautified the horizon in front of him and beside him. The morning sun, slowly rising behind him, painted a slice of treetops that extended from his far right to his far left. Joe became elated and enthralled, forgetting about high gas prices. He was filled with a deep sense of awe, as he immersed his senses in the rich panoply of vivid colours. His awe gave way to humbleness, bordering on a reverent fear.

He had to fight his emotions to keep the car in control. He had a fleeting glimpse that nature's magnificent beauty was arrayed at that moment just for him—not for the hundreds of other drivers who jostled and grabbed for the road. Specifically for him. "But that's silly!" he jolted himself into realizing. "Why me? Or is it a sign?" Yes—a confirmation that talking with Claire was the right thing to do. She was perhaps the only person that he knew who would not ridicule him for finding a confirmation in the glow of a sunrise.

A rude driver gave him another jolt. Yes, reality was back, ugly colours, not gorgeous ones.

Why are gas prices so high?

It seemed to Joe that everyone was complaining. And not just about gas. Ridiculous grocery prices. Surly customer service clerks. Rude drivers. Life was getting tougher and tougher.

And this was supposed to be the best country in the world to live in!

Joe could feel a mood developing among his neighbours, friends, ... actually it seemed like everyone. He was getting worried about the short tempers and the sense that people were just on the verge of lashing out. He even felt guilty about owning a car, as if he were the enemy somehow. He was worried that he might find a rock through his window one night.

And he was worried that he might become one of those rock throwers, just venting his frustration on some random target. Taking out his rage. Responding to some gut instinct.

Things just shouldn't be this way. This was a decent town. A civil country. People were nice.

But the mood had been building for many years. And not only in Joe's generation. His parents had told him that

Why Are Gas Prices So High?

they, too, would grumble about rising gas prices and lowering civility in society.

Was it television? Religion? Politics? What?

What caused gas prices to keep going up?

Joe wished that he had paid more attention in economics lectures. As for the other engineers in his class, he had to take an economics course. He had barely squeaked by, not understanding what was covered. Yes, he wished that he understood the economics of gas pricing.

He felt helpless and frustrated, like he was being dragged along by some unseen tidal force that was inevitable, unstoppable, and overwhelming. And the worst feeling of all was that he couldn't do anything about it.

The best he could do was to try to guess when the gas stations were just about to make a big jump in their prices (simultaneously—Damn!), following their relentless sawtooth pattern, slowly dropping a bit each day, and then suddenly jumping overnight, often higher than before, creeping upward. Yes, try to guess when it would jump, and buy gas just before the jump.

But it seemed that those devious gas companies were clever enough to time their jumps just when most people had gas tanks that were half-full.

Joe Carboni had never really grown up. At least he had not adapted to some of the cruel realities of the world. Life had been too easy for him. Even though he would never admit it, he was spoiled, to some extent. He was happily married, with two children, and living in a nice house, but he was still remarkably innocent.

"If you deliver what you say you will deliver," his first boss had told him, "nobody will be impressed. What's really impressive is if you deliver more than you had promised, or faster, or cheaper."

What an impression that statement had made on him! He carried it through many jobs. But why had it taken him so long in life, all the way up to his first job, to learn something so fundamental?

Even earlier, his Grade 12 English teacher had shown the class how to use a dictionary. How startling was that lesson! Why so late in his education? Why did he need to be taught? Binary search: divide the dictionary in half, then quarters, scan the running headers for page contents, and so on. Joe remembered that lesson more vividly than Wordsworth's poetry or Shakespeare's plays.

Why was he so impressionable? Earlier still, in Grade 9, Joe heard about Jesus Christ and his birth in History class. He was astounded! That's for Church, isn't it? How can they discuss that in school? That was confusing. The world had started to become blurred for him; the neat compartments of knowledge were starting to overlap.

And even in elementary school, he was astonished when a teacher had told the class that they should be polite to their parents. The astonishment was not due to this good advice, but to where it was coming from. Weren't teachers supposed to teach things like arithmetic and geography and spelling? But not how to behave in your family!

After studying computer engineering in university, in which everything was either 1 or 0, on or off, black or white, Joe gradually realized that his childhood view of the world may not be so bad after all, and that his confusion was understandable. The world was not organized as 1s and 0s, but as a large number of overlapping and inter-related topics. He seemed to be the only one who was confused by the overlap among disciplines: history overlapping with religion, family conduct overlapping with school teaching,

Why are gas prices so high?

and so on. Others didn't seem to be bothered. So his earlier discomfort and feelings of paranoia gradually faded away. He became comfortable with who he was. It was OK to be different.

And high gas prices, rude drivers, and surly customer service clerks became part of his life.

"What's to be done?" he asked himself. Politician after politician promised to do something about gas prices, but nothing substantial ever really happened. Joe wondered whether he could do anything about them.

His thoughts received still another jolt, when he suddenly realized that his exit was just ahead. Joe had to forget about pricy gas, tense drivers, and sunny glows for now, in order to concentrate on his own driving and on this upcoming workday.

21

CHAPTER 2 — *Drive the speed limit*

"Why are gas prices so high?"

Joe was moaning, grumbling about his pet peeve, as usual.

"Because you pay those prices," responded Claire. She and Joe were chatting downtown, at one of their regular lunch meetings. She had guessed that he would bring up his usual topic, and she had given some thought to it.

"Huh? Of course I pay the prices—that's what it costs!"

Why Are Gas Prices So High?

"No, it's not like that," said Claire. "Price has nothing to do with cost. If I had a bucket full of gas, and I wanted to sell some of it to you, and you wanted to buy it from me, we would negotiate a price that we would both be content with."

Joe agreed, "Uh, huh!"

"And if you didn't like my price, you would simply leave and shop elsewhere, perhaps at my neighbour's."

"But suppose your neighbour charged the same price?"

"Then you would have three choices, wouldn't you. First, you could give up and pay that price. Second, you could set up your own gas business and charge people what you like. And third ..."

Claire paused, trying to recall something that flashed into her mind that Jane had mentioned earlier that morning.

"And third, ... uh ... you could reduce your gas consumption by ... changing your lifestyle."

This last idea was an inspiration. Claire had felt an intuitive urge to suggest that third option. Even though she hadn't thought it through fully, and felt that she was taking a risk, she offered it anyway. Long ago, she had learned to trust her intuition.

There it is again! thought Claire. It was happening more and more often lately. "Why was it so unpredictable? Arbitrary, one might say. Sporadic. And yet, how very appropriate and trustworthy." Claire looked up to the ceiling, and then gazed out the window, so that Joe wouldn't see her eyes going so blank. She knew that she must look very distracted now. The buzz of a thousand voices took over inside her head. No—not really voices, but ideas. Swirling thoughts. Possibilities. Fantasies. Futures.

Joe had no idea what was going on. Or at least Claire hoped not. If he had any glimpse into how her mind was so mixed up, how her cool logic of "You would have three choices," was only an outward masking of a myriad of sudden, unexpected, inward turbulences ... if he suspected that, would he drop the friendship? What if her boss found out? Or her colleagues? Would she be jeopardizing her career if she revealed how her mind worked? How it wasn't logical thinking that gave her ideas of how to solve problems or to make decisions. No, not logic ... but intuition and inspiration.

Why Are Gas Prices So High?

Joe thought for a moment, and then said, "Yeah! Pay their price! That's what we all do all the time!"

Claire kept quiet, to let Joe think.

"What do you mean by reducing my consumption?"

Good! He bit.

What was it that Jane had said? Claire felt desperate now.

"Well," she began. "If you bought less of my gas, I would reduce its price and charge you less."

"Huh?" This strange logic surprised Joe.

Claire continued. "I would charge less, because I would be stuck with an inventory of gas, and a lower price would encourage my customers to buy it."

"Slow down a moment." Joe thought about such a situation. *Yeah, supply and demand.* "OK, that seems reasonable," he admitted to Claire.

Yes! That's it, thought Claire, *"Slow Down And Live."* Jane had been singing that phrase this morning at breakfast.

Drive the speed limit

It was from some TV commercial, or a song, that she couldn't quite remember. *Yes, that was it!*

"And you can easily use less gas by driving more slowly," she explained. Her inspiration was leading her along now. She felt excited. "Suppose that you slowed down and drove at or slightly below the speed limit all of the time. My guess is that you would then be driving, say, 15 or 20% slower than currently. So, to a first approximation, you would use about 15 or 20% less gas."

"Yeah, but—"

"Let me continue," Claire interjected. "Now, if everyone drove at the speed limit, think of the pressure that would put on the gas companies! The demand for gas would drop sharply. Prices would drop dramatically! We could change the world!"

They talked on for a while, between mouthfuls of their tuna sandwich plates. The gas price topic had led to the speed limit topic, which led to market forces, which led to another topic, and another. But Joe could not get his mind off the idea of driving the speed limit. It was an intriguing idea—but it was too stupid ever to work. *Fascinating, but unrealistic!* he thought.

And yet, compelling.

Much like the sunrise glowing in deep colours on the trees, Joe found deep recesses of his mind brightened and awakened by the notion of driving the speed limit. Amid the turmoil of many topics of discussion, Joe felt drawn to the brightness of this new idea. His rational mind rejected it. But his inner self was warmed by it.

For her part, Claire felt relieved to have verbalized the idea that her intuition had inspired in her. It was not a bad idea, this time. Very often she felt like rejecting her intuitive flashes immediately. But this one seemed fairly straightforward. After all, "Slow down. Use less gas. Prices drop." That seemed wholly reasonable. She was anxious to get out of the restaurant, to breathe the fresh air, and to try out her idea. She was preoccupied with this new revelation, and energized by it.

CHAPTER 3 — *Becoming a believer*

"What trite silliness!"

"Ha!" thought Joe, that evening. "Imagine *me* driving the speed limit!"

His glow had faded back into dullness.

When Claire had suggested the idea, Joe had almost laughed, but he had choked it back and mumbled some decent response, such as "That's an interesting idea." Yes, he had felt strangely drawn to the idea, but his main reaction had been one of ridicule.

Why Are Gas Prices So High?

So now that he was back home, he tried to forget the lunch with Claire. He poured a beer, a Labatt's 50 Ale. *Ah! 50 ... Sounds like a speed limit. Nah! Forget it!* he thought. He took a sip of beer. *And yet, there's something strange. Fifty? No way I could slow down to fifty!* "Seventy, maybe," he said out loud. But ... there was something haunting and seductive about the idea. It sort of got under his skin.

Recalling the sunrise and his feelings of brightness about the speed limit idea, Joe decided to give it a try the next day. He felt very self-conscious, going so slowly, with cars pulling out to pass him, zooming by with indignant drivers, one of whom actually gave him the finger. Joe felt like returning the rudeness, but he kept his cool and speeded up a little.

On the way home, he tried it again—for a while longer.

Then some more the next day.

Amazing! he thought. *This feels good! I feel like I'm doing something about gas prices.*

Three days later, he called Claire to say how the speed limit habit was growing on him.

"Yeah! I tried it, too." responded Claire.

Joe was taken aback. "Really?" he asked. "I thought you had been driving the speed limit for some time."

"No," Claire replied. "I just thought of the idea over our lunch last week. But I like it. I feel much more relaxed."

Joe thought for a moment. Then he offered, "Yeah! Me too. I wonder if you've hit upon something here."

"No, it's no big deal," she replied, puzzled about why Joe was making a fuss.

"Let's talk again in a few days. That will make it more than a week since we started." Joe was intrigued now.

"OK. I'll call you Thursday evening."

Suspecting that they may be onto something big, Joe suggested, "Let's not tell anyone about this yet—Let's experiment with our own reactions for a while."

- - -

They both found it difficult to keep quiet, after another several days of slowing down their driving habits. Claire was caught up in a strange sense of being nudged along by some primal force, like standing in waist-deep water at the beach and feeling tugged out to sea by the gentle undercurrent that followed each surging wave.

She knew what to expect. These feelings had come up from within her on other occasions. But this one was more subtle, and more deep. And more grand and beautiful.

Over the years, Claire had come to recognize these feelings, and to treasure them. She called them "flowing," to put a name to the sense of being carried along by her surroundings, pushed by the wind, or pulled by tidal waters. Not a rough push or pull, or a buffeting by wind or water—but a very gentle flowing. Not a physical sensation, but a contented ambiance that life was unfolding intentionally and that she was an integral part of that process.

When Claire felt her flowing sensations, perhaps three or four times per year, she had learned to savour them. They were precious to her, and they helped to keep her sane and enthusiastic about life. She even imagined that her sense of flowing was part of her identity—part of what made her unique.

Claire believed that flowing was in response to her years of meditation and prayer. She was not a religious person, but very deeply spiritual. Flowing, for her, was a spiritual practice. As she would feel the gentle tug of flowing, she would say a brief prayer, offering herself to whatever service was needed by the cosmos, and then she would flow.

That afternoon, after talking with Joe, she became aware of the unmistakable urge to flow—a subtle urge, but having great power. She was in her car, so she pulled over to a peaceful park, and stopped under some trees. She quieted down her mind and breathed her prayer, "Dear God. I feel your call. I offer myself to whatever service you need. Please guide me." And then she flowed. Gradually, she saw things differently. She seemed to rise up, or to see from some higher place. She saw herself, or at least her body, surrounded by a white glow, at the centre of something very big, enormous, perhaps even the whole world. It was scary for her, but at the same time she felt peaceful. Indeed, she felt profoundly peaceful. This is where she was meant to be. What a beautiful feeling!

It lasted only for a few minutes, but Claire would later recall that she had felt as if she had spent hours flowing in that lovely state.

She gradually came down and seemed to re-enter her body. She became aware of breathing again, and of the warmth of her car, and of sounds of distant traffic.

"Oh, thank you, God," she mouthed softly. "That was beautiful!"

Immediately, it became clear to her that this flowing experience was an affirmation to her that driving the speed limit was the right thing to do, and that she had a vital role in spreading the word as much as possible. She felt strangely excited. She didn't understand why she was so excited, but she knew enough about her feelings to trust them, especially when she had these flowing experiences.

So she started to tell others about the notion of slowing down to drive the speed limit.

- - -

Joe also felt excited, and, in his case, he knew why. He had developed a habit of trying to understand his feelings.

Only recently had he even admitted that he had feelings. Before that, he tended to ignore his emotions, or he tried to control them. He viewed it as a sign of weakness if he was not able to keep his feelings under strict control.

But he had one of those life-changing experiences about five years ago. He lost an important job competition to a younger, less experienced person, and he took it hard. He considered the loss as his own fault, he felt very inadequate, and he suffered a mild depression.

Fortunately for him, a counsellor asked him about his feelings.

"Feelings?" asked Joe. "I don't have feelings!"

So began a year or so of counselling, which helped Joe start on a road to experiencing all sorts of emotions. But he still retained a form of control by wanting to understand why he had those feelings.

"OK, I feel sad about this, or I love the beauty of that, or that other thing thrills me—but I need to understand why I feel sad, or why some things are beautiful to me, or why others give me thrills."

Joe's form of comfort was to acknowledge his emotions, but to study them objectively. That was a good start, suggested his counsellor, and it seemed to work for him.

So he felt a delicious excitement about Claire's speed limit idea. He could see a macroscopic connection between

Why Are Gas Prices So High?

the individual act of one person driving the speed limit on the lowest extreme, and a global lessening of air pollution on the highest extreme. And somewhere in between these extremes, he could see gas prices dropping, due to a lessening demand. But the important thing for him was making the mental leap to that top level, well beyond lower gas prices, up to the level of cleaner air. Merely forcing gas prices down was not exciting for Joe. Yes, it would provide some relief for his frustration with high gas prices, but No, it would never catch on. It was simply too small a step, or not appealing enough to the great unwashed masses, or perhaps it would be too hard to sell.

Intriguing, yes, but not exciting.

On the other hand, cleaning up the atmosphere ... now that's exciting!

Yes, Claire had hit upon a brilliant idea. But how could we spread the word?

Joe decided to tell a few people, to test the idea. A few phone calls here, a few email messages there.

CHAPTER 4 *Trying something new*

Jean-Marc Métivier felt strangely peaceful.

As he drove calmly through the countryside around Clermont-Ferrand in central France, observing the trees and the clouds, he reflected on this unusual feeling. Driving slowly, at the speed limit, calmed him down. And was he ever ready to be calmed down!

His doctor had warned Jean-Marc to slow down his hectic pace of life. With warnings of high blood pressure, heart attacks, and strokes, the doctor had expressed great concern for his patient. This time Jean-Marc had taken the

Why Are Gas Prices So High?

warning seriously. But where to cut back? How to slow down? His life was so full, and so complicated, and everything was so urgent—pressures of family, business, two mistresses—he needed to speed up, not slow down, just to keep his sanity.

And then an amazing thing had happened. Jean-Marc received an email message from a colleague. It had been forwarded from a friend of a friend, from some guy named Joe Carboni, advocating the benefits of driving the speed limit in order to save money on gas. A bird chirped. A phrase of a pleasant sonata drifted into the room. The sun illuminated his computer monitor. The mood was right for not ignoring the email message. *Why not?* Jean-Marc thought. *Maybe I'll give it a try!*

That evening, as he drove, cars zoomed past him. But one car seemed to be keeping pace with him. Jean-Marc and the other driver exchanged glances, smiles, and thumbs-up signs. And then he was hooked!

So there he was, a few weeks later, driving home in a leisurely manner, reflecting, anxious to see his wife and children, smiling about the phone calls and email messages and conversations he had that day, urging others also to try driving the speed limit.

Trying something new

- - -

Texas is so vast, so long and flat and straight!

Why would such a great land generate such urgency and rudeness and impatience in its residents? Amanda Patterson turned over this question in her mind. She was the most rude and impatient person she knew, and the one always in the biggest hurry. She would routinely cut off drivers and make rude gestures if she did not like their driving style. A pretty Texan blonde, tall, slender, and fashionable like a model, she worked long hours as a computer programmer, she had men clamouring for her, and she partied hard. She understood now, as part of her thinking about peoples' urgency and impatience, how she had been sucked into the fast pace of a young professional's life in an affluent society.

But Amanda had felt that something was missing. Some troubling emptiness in her heart had a life of its own and spoke to her. It was getting hard to ignore its plaintive voice.

Months went by. A year. More months.

Then, over a beer after work, at her friends' regular bar in Richardson, just north of Dallas, she met a man who won her over at their very first eye contact. She was infatuated, and in love immediately.

The only problem was that he was a slow driver, having recently heard of how driving the speed limit could save money and generate less air pollution. Amanda hated driving with him. They argued about their two driving styles. But within a month, during which all other aspects of their relationship were top-notch, she decided to give in and try it herself.

And soon Amanda was hooked. Drive slowly. Speed limit. Rudeness. Speed up ... No! Slow down again. Ignore them. This is *my* life! Try it again the next day. Take the back roads—the less-travelled routes. Slow down. Yes ... hear the birds and the breeze.

"I like it!" Amanda replied to her inner voice.

And being very influential in her circle of friends, and beyond, Amanda did not keep quiet about her new lifestyle. Within a few weeks—a month at most—she had hundreds of people driving the speed limit. And they all loved it, too.

- - -

Ah! What a glorious weekend!

Trying something new

Hal Wagstone basked in the memories of one of his best yachting weekends ever. The weather had been superb. His crew performed admirably. And his boat had been an extension of his body.

He was driving back from Dunedin, on the south-east coast of New Zealand, on a Sunday evening, to his home in Queenstown. Ordinarily, he could do the trip in about two and a half hours, zipping along Highway 8, loving the rush of mountain curves alternating with long straight stretches. How many times had he driven this route? Too many! It was time to move to Dunedin, so that he could enjoy the open sea every day, not just on weekends. If only his job would let him move.

His job. What a bummer! Gorgeous weekend. But now the stress would start to rise, right on schedule, as he felt Monday morning's approach.

But would it rise this evening? This trip was different. Hal was trying something new ... driving the speed limit all the way. Yes, it would take him half an hour longer, but it was worth a try.

Out on that glorious sea, sipping a beer, chatting with his crew members and friends, Hal was astonished to hear of an idea that had never occurred to him: driving at the speed limit. One of the guys said that he had read of it in a newspaper, as originating in Canada, and recommended for reducing gas consumption and stress. Hal was immediately struck by the idea, and resolved to try it on his drive back to Queenstown.

And try it, he did! It took a bit of getting used to, but Hal persisted, being captivated by the notion of reducing his stress as he headed toward Monday. He had to remind himself frequently to relax his foot from the gas pedal. But fortunately, on this single-lane highway, he encountered many other drivers who seemed to be out for a leisurely Sunday evening drive, and this time he decided not to rush past them, but to join them in their leisure.

And, yes, the trip did take just over three hours.

The good news was that the timing had been right for Hal to hear about this new idea of being more relaxed. After many years of running in the rat race, he was open to suggestions for slowing down.

It was clear to Hal that he had discovered a new lifestyle, that he would find a way to move to Dunedin in the near future, and that he would tell many others of his newfound way to achieve calmness and peace.

- - -

Monica George was more nervous than she had ever remembered being.

Her turn was next, and she wished that she could just fade out, and quietly disappear.

But, no, she was next on the agenda. And she had asked to speak to the group. Nobody was forcing her to do it. This was her idea. And even though she was not an activist or a public speaker, Monica had to admit that speaking to her Nursery School parent's night monthly meeting was not that great a risk. After all, these were friendly people, not hostile enemies. And she wasn't asking for money or votes or a sale. She simply wanted to tell her story, to share her excitement of a new idea with people who would give her a sympathetic audience.

"What I want to tell you in my five minutes is about a wonderful new lifestyle choice that I am trying, and want to recommend to you all." Monica wondered why she had been nervous. The twenty or so other mothers, and a few fathers, were all smiling and attentive. She knew most of them by name. This was a good audience to start her public speaking career with: a group of parents in suburban Calgary, Alberta.

"A couple of weeks ago, Mark and I decided to try slowing down our lives a bit. We realized that we were not setting good examples for our children, and especially now that Kendra is coming to this wonderful school, and we see her imitating so many of our actions and choices, we were looking for ways to be more responsible parents and citizens.

"Then we discovered a really neat idea that was innovated by a lady out east: driving the speed limit! It seems so silly that we didn't even think of it ourselves. But it hit us like a light turning on. Yes! That's exactly what we wanted!"

Monica made the mistake of pausing briefly to look at some of the faces. A few people smiled, a few raised their eyebrows, but a few avoided her eyes, looking at their feet, shuffling with embarrassment, glancing at their watches.

Mark had coached her in advance that she might get such a mixture of reactions, and he had taught her the trick of glancing at her own watch, making a joke about how she

Trying something new

must hurry so not to take too much time, and chuckling to herself to relieve tension.

She was able to mount a courageous battle against her inner demon. "So we tried driving more slowly," she continued. "We soon realized that we were not only saving gas, but also taking action in areas that we had long believed in. We were doing something positive about generating less pollution, we were showing others, especially our children, that we wanted a scaled-back lifestyle, and we were beginning to feel more peaceful and calm."

The passion in her voice and her manner caught the attention of the clockwatchers in the room. They were listening now, attentively.

She talked for a few minutes about their family decision, and about her feelings that came from driving more slowly. Then she concluded. "So let me recommend to you, with all sincerity, that you try it for yourselves. Try driving the speed limit for a while. Our thought is that you will like it. Our guess is that you will become more calm in your daily lives—and for sure, we all could use some more calmness—and our bet is that you'll be anxious to tell lots of others."

CHAPTER 5 — *The word spreads*

Three months!

Has it only been three months?

Joe was waiting for Claire at their usual restaurant. It was not with impatience and annoyance that he waited. It was with excitement and enthusiasm. In fact, he was glad that she was late, for it gave him the opportunity to gather his thoughts and savour the moment.

What mood is this? Joe wondered. *Have I really become this relaxed? How light I feel! Janet calls me serene. Me, serene! Who would have thought? Am I ever*

Why Are Gas Prices So High?

glad we told the others! Who would have guessed it would catch on so rapidly?

Joe felt comfortable inside his skin for the first time in many years ... perhaps for the first time in his life. That comfort was obvious to others, especially his wife.

Even the cats came now to sit on his lap. He found time to help his children with their homework. He became more romantic with Janet. His neighbour expressed delight in seeing him puttering in the yard. His workroom was less cluttered ... his life was less cluttered.

All because he was driving the speed limit now!

Yes, it took longer to get where he was going. But he found that he was going to fewer places. Or less often. Or less frantically.

He would plan out his route more carefully, and he would choose to buy less, or to rush less, or to take the bus occasionally, just for the fun of it.

Yes, savour the moment! And savour the anticipation of the surprise that he had planned for Claire.

The word spreads

"Hey, there, thoughtful person!" she greeted him, approaching the table.

"Hi, Claire! Thought-filled, to be more precise. My mind is racing!"

"No," Claire replied, as she sat down. *"Thoughtful.* You saved the good seat for me. I really like that! You truly have changed."

Joe smiled, not only to see his friend, but also to realize that he had quite unconsciously chosen the inward-facing seat, to let her have the nicer view, for the first time ever. Wow! It happened without his even realizing it!

"Can you believe what's happening?" he changed the subject. "This morning I got four email messages asking who Claire Atwater was, this genius who suggested driving the speed limit!"

"Oh, come on, now!" Claire was embarrassed that Joe kept telling people that she had come up with the idea. "I wish you would stop telling people that I started it."

Joe brushed off her objections, "Too late now. The movement has a life of its own. Did you see the article in *The Economist* yet?"

49

"What article? They interviewed me last week. Did they print something?"

"Yup! Here it is." Joe passed over his copy, with the page opened to the brief article 'Slow down and save.' "Hot off the press!"

Claire scanned the column, while Joe beamed at her. The magazine reported a worldwide spread of a new conservation movement: driving the speed limit for the purpose of saving gas, but having the unexpected side-effect of enabling people to slow down their lives, to become more relaxed, and to become more civil. They attributed the starting of the movement to Claire Atwater. A sociologist that they interviewed explained that people were ready for a grassroots change of a fundamental nature, and predicted society's saving. Where governments, NGOs, and UN conferences had failed, the common folk succeeded. A scientist predicted less pollution. A clergyman predicted spiritual renewal. An economist predicted that gas prices would dip even further, but then rebound. A skeptic predicted disappointment with another new fad. A media guru noted that such a movement could only catch on so rapidly with modern network communications. The article concluded with typical fence-sitting, offering hope, but a wait-and-see attitude.

The word spreads

"Wow! This is amazing!" Claire was obviously delighted and astonished. "I can't wait to show this to Peter and the girls!"

"I thought not, so here's a copy for you."

"Oh! You're amazing, Joe. Thank you! Did you really buy an extra copy?"

Their enthusiasm was interrupted by a waiter's arrival to take their order. "I can't even think of eating now," Claire said.

"Well, let's have a quick lunch, and then get ready for what happens next," suggested Joe, realizing that Claire was bound for global exposure.

- - -

After they had ordered, they both kept quiet for a moment, allowing their thoughts to emerge, to tumble, and to thrive.

Claire's thoughts were myriad. Did she want this fame and glory? All she had been doing was following her intuition. She had no grand schemes of saving the world. Sure, she had heard the maxim 'Think globally, act locally.' Yes, she composted and recycled and supported charities that promoted ecology and sustainability. She tried to teach the girls about caring for the environment. She prayed for world peace and for proper stewardship of the earth. She even tried to visualize the earth with an unpolluted atmosphere, and she meditated on that image. But somehow she had never imagined that she could make a difference. After all, she was just a small-town girl. And Canadian. What could she do? She would look after her little corner of the world. She worried about fame. Lack of privacy. Threats to the girls. Unlisted phone numbers. Would friends desert her? Perhaps it all would pass, and life wouldn't change. But maybe ... maybe the change was OK. Yes, even in her own life, she had become more peaceful. And those dreams! Those daydreams and flashes of inspiration! Quieting down her mind, by slowing down her life, seemed to have prompted an awakening of her intuition. She was already fairly intuitive, and had her flowing experiences, but this was amazing! Frightening ... She saw a bigger picture now, much bigger. That first thought of driving the speed limit, which she had verbalized to Joe a few months ago, that thought was indeed inspired! *I'm so glad I slowed down so I could hear ....*

All this in a moment or two, while life and bustle in the restaurant went on.

The word spreads

Joe, for his part, juggled many thoughts also. Janet was so beautiful. How wonderful to love your wife, and to find her enthrallingly beautiful! She nurtured a charming household—children, garden, wonderful home. How did he get so lucky? Here with Claire, also very enticing, he still thought of Janet. Was it only now? Did he just now realize it? Had his wandering eye only now come home? Who could have predicted that slowing down to drive the speed limit would let him realize how beautiful his wife was? How proud he was of his children? How wonderful a home they had? To Hell with the naysayers! He had found more important values. Let them taunt. Let them learn, or not learn ... what did it matter? What a sense of freedom, of unburdening, an inner cleansing! Society had become so outward-focused, so externally-driven. And he had become so caught up in it. Are others so depraved as he had become? Depraved. Yes, the opposite of 'praved.' He smiled at coining a new word. What potential he felt! What a future! What hope! How amazingly God works! It's like poetry, or like dreams. The obvious can't be stated directly—it must be hinted at, portrayed symbolically, a mood created. "How many messages have I missed?" he wondered. "How often do we not see the obvious? Oh! If only it's not too late, to let each individual person discover the truth from within. If only they also will slow down and listen ... and respond."

- - -

"Excuse me. Is your name Claire?"

Their reverie was interrupted by another customer, a girl who had been watching them. "I want to congratulate you and thank you for starting the L-movement!"

"L-movement? What's that?" Claire responded, jolted out of her thoughts. Perhaps the girl had mistaken her for someone else.

"You know: Limits! Liberation! Life!" the girl beamed a smile, and held up her hand to form the letter 'L' by pointing her finger upwards and her thumb outwards. "We all love your 'speed limit' idea, and we use this sign to remind each other to slow down. Everyone's doing it! Even the chat rooms are full of the L-sign! To think that it started in our home town! Way cool!

"The L-sign used to mean *Loser*," the girl explained, "but somehow everyone knows that when you flash it with a smile, it now means 'Slow down and enjoy life!' And we have you to thank for starting it all!"

The word spreads

Claire was a bit disoriented. Clearly this young lady was enthusiastic, but Claire was confused. How could this be happening?

"I'll leave you to your lunch, but may I have your autograph? My friends will be so envious!"

Claire signed the paper and shook her hand. "Oh my God! It's happening!" she thought. She looked around. Two or three people were flashing the L-sign as a greeting or on departing. A life of its own—yes! It was totally out of her hands now.

"See?" Joe said. "It spread like wildfire! I'm glad we waited a week or two before telling others. I wanted to convince myself that I was changing, simply by driving the speed limit, before spreading the word."

"Yeah, I guess so." Claire mouthed, hesitantly. "Uh! ... Yes, I had felt a change, too. Then we both told others."

"I remember picking people carefully. Not everyone was ready for the idea." Joe was retrospective. "Then I sent a few email messages. And I did a posting to a Website that promoted sustainable development."

"Same here. I told a few people, and I suppose they told others. A few email messages. And then I started getting messages back, some from people that you had told. I remember being angry at you for giving out my name and address."

"But you were the one. You came up with the idea." Joe never wavered from his acknowledgment of Claire's role in starting the movement.

Claire shuddered, feeling a chill. "And then it was gone. A life of its own, as you said. I still can't believe that three months—actually only two and a half months—was enough for the word to spread by person, phone, email, websites, ... Holy smoke! People must have been ready!"

Joe recalled his own frustration with gas prices a few months ago. "For sure! People were ready. Who knows, the word may not have spread a year earlier, or a year later."

CHAPTER 6   *Backlash*

"Balderdash!

"You granola-crunching, slacker-filled hippies out there. You make me sick! Speed limits are for losers! Speed limits are for you lefty-socialist, welfare-bummed, second-class namby-pambies who couldn't make a dime if you fell over one. My God! What's happening to our mixed-up world? OK, folks. I'll take just one more caller on this topic, and then we're gonna switch to something more important!"

Why Are Gas Prices So High?

Luke Brookside was fuming. His talk show attracted a huge following. It's a wonder that he hadn't had a heart attack years ago, from high blood pressure. "Hello, John. You're on the air."

"Good morning, Luke. I partly agree with you."

"PARTLY? Come on, John. Make it Full Agreement!"

"Well, let me explain. You, of all people, are trying to teach your listeners to think for themselves, so surely you can allow us to agree partly and still have our own ..."

"Yeah! Yeah! What's your point, John? Get to the point!"

"OK. Well, let me ask you, Luke, whether you have tried for yourself driving the speed limit?"

"Oh! Get serious! Haven't you heard me say that speed limits are for wimps?"

John was patient. He knew that the slightest indication of exasperation or annoyance in his voice would prompt Luke to cut him off immediately, dismissing him as a "lefty."

Why did people keep calling in to Luke's program? They were usually abused if they showed the slightest hesitation, or if they expressed liberal views, or if he guessed that they would waste time. But they seemed to enjoy that abuse.

Much of Luke's appeal was due to how much sense he made. He cut to the heart of each matter, and treated every issue as black and white.

"Well, I tried it. And I love it," John said. "You see, it's something that doesn't become clear until you try it."

"Really! One of those airy-fairy mystical things, is it?" broke in Luke.

John ignored him. "On the surface, it seems like the benefit of slowing down to the speed limit is just using less gas. And if everyone did that, the gas companies would have extra gas on their hands, so they would have to reduce their prices. And it would seem that prices would bounce back up once the demand picks up again. But the neat thing is that the demand won't pick up again."

Luke did his sarcastic thing once more, "Oh, here we go with the wishy-washy nonsense again!"

Why Are Gas Prices So High?

He still couldn't get a rise out of John. "What happens is that people truly lower their consumption level. They become satisfied with a scaled-down life. Call it mystical, if you like, but people feel some attunement with nature, with the under-developed nations, with the limited resources we have, and they adjust their lifestyles ... "

"C'mon, John! Are you telling me that I'm gonna slow down because some loser in some far-off country needs more money?"

John paused for a moment to collect his thoughts. "If that's your view of the world, Luke, then it's becoming clear to me how the world got this way. Give us a chance, will you? If you want to drive your vehicle the way you always have done, then OK. But there's a whole ton of us who want to give the world a chance to recover, and to bounce back, so we would appreciate your letting us do so. Good-bye."

A hangup. Luke got a hangup! That never happens! He always cuts off the callers, or dismisses them with a curt remark. But John hung up on him first, before he got the chance.

Backlash

"Well, folks, that was John!" he explained, trying to sound unfazed by having someone else hang up on him. "Let's hope his numbers are dwindling. As I've stated many times, this country, indeed the whole western world, has become great through growth, growth, and more growth. All these lily-livered cowards want us to shrink, shrink, and shrink, all the way back to living in caves. Well, not while I'm around. I'll fight them in the streets. I'll fight them on the airwaves! I'll fight them at the gas pumps! I'll show them which finger to point upwards!"

This was Luke Brookside's way, blustering, reactionary, even to the point of being redneck. People loved his show, in a sort of love/hate way. He held some extreme views, usually of a common-sense nature, but sometimes seeming to be controversial just for controversy's sake.

"This is truly amazing, folks. What's the world coming to? In all my years .... Well, that's the end of that topic for today. Let's take a break, and when we return, I want to hear your views on the other topics that I introduced at the start of the show. We'll be right back!"

The program cut to some commercials. Luke popped a pill and swallowed it with a long drag of strong, black coffee. He sat back and sighed, wondering briefly how

Why Are Gas Prices So High?

much longer he could keep up this pace. What's the world coming to, indeed! There seemed to be so very much to teach. Was he the only voice of sanity in the whole city? The whole country?

Every year it seemed to be getting worse. Luke couldn't retire ... there was still so much to do, so much to teach!

Part B: Two Years Ago

CHAPTER 7 — *Newton's third law*

A year after Claire had come up with her speed limit idea, the world was a greatly changed place.

All sorts of people around the world had adopted the speed limit idea within a couple of months. Huge numbers of drivers were ready for a change, anxious for something new, looking for some way to act and to make a change. All it needed was a simple idea to be introduced, a catalyst for a super-saturated solution, and driving habits were changed around the world, almost overnight.

Why Are Gas Prices So High?

And the changes persisted. It was clearly not just a new fad. People felt good about slowing down their driving habits. It seemed that they really wanted to contribute somehow.

But slowing down their cars was not enough.

"Did you read about this group of people in Switzerland who are creating fifty percent less garbage?" Claire asked.

The Atwater family was sitting in their den, reading, on a Sunday evening. It was one of their family customs. Every Sunday evening was family time. They would tell each other what was happening in their lives, they would read together, they would share stories, bounce ideas around, and generally be together. They didn't watch television, unless they all agreed on some educational or cultural program that they all would benefit from. Peter and Claire had even been known to postpone business trips to very late Sunday evening or Monday morning, so not to miss one of their family times.

The girls realized that they had something special, and unusual, here. Their friends knew not to phone them on Sunday evenings.

Mary asked, "How do they do that?"

Her mother responded, half reading from the article, "It would seem that they shop carefully to buy things that have less packaging, they compost everything they can, and they grind up garbage with a compactor into smaller bags than they had used before."

"Neat!" said Jane. "I heard of a family that got their garbage down to only one or two bags per year!"

"Yeah! Ginormous bags!" laughed Mary.

"But it doesn't count," Peter observed, "Unless you get an organized group of people cooperating on some conservation or saving venture."

"Right! Like Mom's L-movement!" Mary waved her hands, flashing the L-sign.

Claire immediately diverted the conversation away from that topic back to her original one. "But it would appear that this one is a group activity."

"Well, good for them," replied Peter. "I hope it catches on. Actually, when you think of it, we do a pretty good job of keeping our garbage down to a minimum."

"Yeah! But you can't flash a 'G' with your fingers," Jane laughed.

"Sure I can," called out Mary, stumbling with various contortions of her hands and fingers, trying to form a 'G.'

After a few chuckles and teasings, they all returned to their readings.

"Hey! Here's an interesting story." Peter leaned forward and folded his newspaper so that the others could read the headline. "Evidently, there's a worldwide movement that started in Italy called 'Slow Cities,' in which a bunch of communities have adopted a commitment to drive slowly and make less noise. It grew out of an earlier movement, 'Slow Food,' as a rebellion against the fast food restaurants that were spreading throughout Europe."

Claire was impressed. "That's neat! So the sentiment behind that movement would condition people to be ready for driving the speed limit."

"Yeah," replied Peter. "And if you can get Italians to slow down, you've solved the world's problems!"

They all read silently for a while.

Newton's third law

Jane looked serious and puzzled. "Mom ... why are so many people against your L-movement?"

"Which ones are you reading about now, Honey?" Claire asked.

"It says here that some union leaders claim that the movement will put their members out of work." Jane's forehead was wrinkled, and her eyes appeared strained. "And the heads of some car companies agree with them."

"Well, at least you're getting unions and management to agree!" quipped Peter.

"It's not a joke, Peter," Claire reprimanded her husband. "This is serious stuff. Jane raises a very good point. Not everyone wants the L-movement to succeed."

Peter was appropriately chastened. "You're right. It seems there will always be people who can't see the big picture, but will always push for their own self-interest."

"But why must that be?" Jane furrowed her brow even more. "Why is the world such a mixed-up place?"

Why Are Gas Prices So High?

"It's just the way it is, Honey," replied her father. "Every time a good idea is brought up, like Mom's, there are always people who come forward to call it a bad idea."

"But why?" Jane pondered a bit.

"You know something?" she said, tentatively. "It's sort of like Newton's Law!"

"Oh? Which one?" asked Peter.

"I think it's the second or third one," answered Jane. "We just studied it in our Science course. You know, something like 'For every action, there's an equal and opposite reaction.' It's a law of physics, but maybe it applies also to personal and social situations."

Everyone paused for a moment, to consider this penetrating insight by the 16-year old young lady of the family.

"Hey! Maybe you've got something there, Jane!" Claire always encouraged the girls to think independently, and to explore new ideas for themselves. "Yes, I've noticed things like that in my own personality, such as when I want to change a habit, like procrastination, something in me resists and pulls me back even more, to putting things off worse than before."

Newton's third law

Immediately, Claire's mind was opened up to reveal many other examples of this "law" in action in her own life. She recalled numerous times that she had drifted into a sort of social laziness and had neglected to contact certain friends for many weeks. Then she would resolve, partly from guilt, partly from a sense of duty, to phone them, or to write to them, or to visit them. But, quite remarkably, some sort of counter-reaction would always result. She might feel a gradually-mounting anxiety that would waken her in the night with sweating and panting. Or she might find herself dropping things in the kitchen, or taking a wrong turn while driving.

Similarly, she would have unusual and unexplainable reactions to any change to long-standing habits, such as the times she started regular abdominal crunches to reduce her belly bulge, or when she resolved to get up a half-hour early each day to meditate and pray. All sorts of barriers seemed to present themselves. Old habits, especially ones of laziness or neglect, were amazingly hard to break.

Her mind raced with delight. Jane's idea just might explain so much for her! If that were the case, then perhaps she was simply experiencing a natural phenomenon, and not some weird quirk in her personality. Perhaps she was healthy, not sick.

Why Are Gas Prices So High?

Peter wanted to add an example of his own, but deferred to Mary, who looked anxious to contribute.

"Me, too," piped up Mary, fourteen years old, hoping that she had an important idea to share. "When I feel like pulling Fluffy's tail, I also feel sorry for her, and want to pat her." She smiled, proud to have added her idea to the conversation.

A wonderful aspect of the family mood that Claire and Peter had created was the lack of doubt in the girls' self-assurance. Mary had not ended her statement with a question mark, looking for validation from her parents. She had simply stated it as a fact.

Peter knew enough not to reward her with a superficial "Good Girl!" remark, attributing a moral value to her opinions, but to treat her like an adult. "Yes, I have reactions like that also, Mary. Like at work, when I tease someone, I feel bad later, worrying that I might have hurt that person's feelings." Similarly, he chose not to point out to Jane that it was Newton's Third Law that she had cited. He was proud of her for at least recognizing that it was one of Newton's laws, and he didn't want to squelch her natural curiosity by correcting some minor point.

Newton's third law

"I wonder, as you said, Jane, if that Law could be extended to social behaviour." Claire was always dazzled by some of the insights coming out of the children. "I can see it in action in my own personality. But for whole classes of people—now, that's intriguing!

"What a great Science project it would make," mused Jane. "You could get groups of people, and probe them with some stimulus that upset their normal state, and observe their reactions."

"Sounds like a Master's Thesis to me," observed Peter.

Slightly tiffed, Claire brought it back to Jane's level. "Yes, it would be a great thing to research. I'll bet you could find a lot of data from reading the newspapers, or history books."

"Good idea," Peter added. "Or biographies of famous people might provide lots of examples of the pendulum swings of social interactions."

"Why not just do it for Mom's L-movement?" This was Mary, once again bringing the topic home, stating the obvious.

Why Are Gas Prices So High?

The short pause that followed provided the silence for them all to hear each other's sharp intakes of breath.

"My God! You're right, Mary!" burst out Peter. "That's brilliant!"

Jane jumped over and hugged her sister. "Coo-welll! Hey, Little Sister! You pull through once again with the best idea of all! I'm going to run with it ... and you'll be the person that I dedicate the project to ... along with Mom and Dad."

"Don't forget Fluffy!" Mary reminded her.

CHAPTER 8 — *Drive the self-limits*

"Jane and I need your help, Joe." Claire had phoned Joe, full of excitement, anxious to get his input.

"Of course!" replied Joe. "Whatever I can do."

"Could you help us with some brainstorming? Jane is doing a school project on society's negative reactions to new ideas for change, and she's focusing on our speed limit idea. What she wants to do is generate a bunch of examples of negative reactions that she can use in her report. She asked me if I would invite you to join us in a brainstorming session."

"Well, sure! That's nice of her to think of asking me. Let's see now ... there are lots of ideas that I can think of, like, the car manufacturers, the oil producers, the towing companies ... in fact, everyone who is comfortable with life as it has evolved, especially if their job depends on maintaining the status quo."

Claire stopped him by suggesting, "Before we get too far, how about lunch with the two of us tomorrow to think of ideas? Jane has the lunchtime free from school."

That sounded like a plan to Joe. "OK. The usual arrangements?"

- - -

Jane had mixed feelings about the meeting. On the one hand, she was happy to think of her mother and one of her colleagues helping her with ideas for the project she was starting. But on the other hand, she had butterflies in her stomach, and second thoughts about opening her idea to Joe's scrutiny. What if it was a stupid idea? What if they could think of nothing to add? How embarrassed she would be if her idea turned out to be a dud! Especially because everyone considered her to be very smart.

Drive the self-limits

Jane hated being smart. Why couldn't she be just normal, like everyone else? Besides, she didn't think she was smart, as many people told her. What did they know? What she admitted to was being curious. Her curiosity about so many things was misinterpreted as smartness.

However, she did recognize how fortunate she was, being curious, and being born into such a great family. But her dominant feeling was one of resentment ... or perhaps embarrassment. Or was it gratitude? Or humility? Jane was more confused than ever. *Do other people have struggles like this?* she wondered. *Surely not!* She looked around at her friends and family, and saw a whole bunch of people who seemed fairly sure of themselves, quite confident about their roles in life.

Perhaps she only thought that other people were confident. She didn't like to get too close to others, for fear that they would see just how insecure she was. So she pretended to be in a class by herself. She wanted to be, or at least pretended to be, above all those human emotions. The world of ideas was what fascinated her and drew her, like a moth to a flame. To her death? Like a burned-up moth? Was that it?

Why Are Gas Prices So High?

Of all the things that Jane hated, she hated most her name. *Jane!* She couldn't even think of her name without inserting the word "Plain" in front: "Plain Jane!" What a curse to have a name like that! By rights, it should not have bothered her. After all, it was just a name. "Names will never hurt me," went the children's rhyme. But why couldn't she have been given an interesting name, such as Kiersten or Adrianna? Furthermore, Jane knew about the Power of The Name. The Angel had wrestled Jacob, but would not reveal his name. God would not reveal his name to Moses. To know someone's name was to have power over him or her. Jane knew all of this. Perhaps if she had not known this bit of psychology or mythology, the name Plain Jane would not bother her. But she did know it. Was it true that a little bit of knowledge was worse than none?

She was anything but plain. Of medium height, with long, full, dark hair, having deep, beautiful, sparkling brown eyes, Jane was quite striking, part way through the transition from awkward teenager to charming young lady. At least her boyfriend, Ron, thought so. And so did many other boys who would have liked to be her boyfriend. But she didn't think so. It was the world of ideas that attracted her, not the latest in fashions or singers or cosmetics. She pretended to be interested in these things, in order to be accepted into her peer group, but the effort to maintain such a front took its toll. Sometimes she would wake up from a troubled sleep, sweating, panting, and anxious.

Jane kept all of this turmoil to herself. Even though her family environment was wonderfully open, with lots of deep discussions about the important things in life, she had her own secret world that she found comfort in occupying.

Over a year ago, she had taken up meditation and exploring her spiritual life. She had followed an inner attraction to some Eastern thought, such as the Dalai Lama's claim to be a reincarnation of previous Dalai Lamas, and the practice of intoning various vowel sounds as mantras for spiritual growth. This exploration was a reaction to a very influential incident that had occurred in her church. An older lady, Sandra, had given an impassioned witness to a group of children about the famous statement in *John* 3:16, "For God so loved the world that he gave his only Son, that whoever believes in him should not perish but have eternal life."

"What rubbish!" Jane had thought to herself, reacting with offence, puzzlement, and guilt. "Why his *only* son? Aren't we *all* children of God, made in his image? What about all the daughters? What was the sense of such a stupid sacrifice? And why is God a *He*? What about those who don't believe in him/her/it? What about those who haven't heard of the Christian message, because they live in other parts of the world or on other planets? What about the millions, or the billions, of innocent people who haven't heard? Are they doomed to perish and not have eternal life? What kind of vengeful, irrational god is that? Why should I 'just have faith,' as Sandra and the others keep saying?" These thoughts had tumbled through Jane's mind, as she struggled with her faith.

Jane had felt sorry for Sandra, that she and so many other people interpreted the Bible literally, and not symbolically, as poetry or myth, to guide the soul. What a waste!

That incident, nearly two years ago, had triggered Jane's conviction that reincarnation and karma offered the best explanation of cosmic principles that she was aware of. If people did not hear about something, such as "the Gospel," or did not experience something, in this life, then they may be given the chance to do so, especially if they strive to advance their own evolution, when they are reborn into a next life. Since that time, even though she was torn with guilt and felt like a deserter or a turncoat, she explored alternate approaches to the Christian myth. She secretly read about Buddhism, mystical spirituality, Taoism, and other such "heretical" topics. She partly hoped that Christianity was right, and that her diverse readings would help her appreciate her own religion.

It was no wonder that she felt turmoil. It was no wonder that she was torn between the external world and her inner spirit.

And yet, her evolution to the point of asking such fundamental questions and feeling such inner urges, her belief that she was different from so many others, these ideas gave her a peaceful confidence as she prepared for the meeting with Joe and her mother.

- - -

At their customary restaurant the next day, having waded through the greetings of "Hi, Claire!" and flashing L-signs, Claire and Jane sat down with Joe.

"Wow! Things are happening fast," Claire observed.

Jane was dazzled.

"Yeah, tell me about it!" Joe responded. He had developed an extensive correspondence, mostly by email and Internet discussion groups, on various subjects associated with the world's sustainable development and conservation. "You should see some of the stuff I've been reading, Jane! If you need some material, I can make lots available."

Jane was impressed with Joe already, and she was thrilled to be having lunch downtown with her mother and one of her colleagues.

After they had ordered their meals, Claire turned them to the topic of her daughter's project. "What do you think of Jane's idea, Joe?"

"So, let me see if I understand," Joe offered. "You're saying that there may be a law of social action, or dynamics, or something, that generates a bad reaction for every good action."

"Yes, something like that," responded Claire. "Although 'opposite' might be better than 'good' and 'bad.' It's actually Jane's idea, and I want to help her with some basic data that she can consider as input to test her theory. Perhaps you could explain, Honey."

Jane felt a bit nervous, not that her idea would be considered silly, but that she would not be able to explain it properly. Her feeling was like stage fright—she was totally confident of her role, but nervous about her performance. "Well, I thought that perhaps we could broaden Newton's Third Law beyond physical systems to personal and social systems."

Joe needed no reminder of what Newton's Third Law was. "Hmm! Very clever! Yes ... Something tells me that Newton already suspected that. 'As above, so below.' Wasn't it he, or some medieval alchemist, who said that?"

"Well, whatever!" Claire retorted, anxious to credit her daughter with the idea, not Newton or someone else, and a bit exasperated with Joe's academic ways. "So could we brainstorm some examples of negative reactions to the speed limit movement?"

Joe considered for a moment. "Well, OK.... So, there are the ideas I mentioned on the phone yesterday. Let's list them.

"First, the car manufacturers won't like the idea of people driving more slowly, because that could mean that cars last longer, through less wear and tear, and thus they would sell fewer new cars."

"Right, and the unions see the movement as reducing the number of manufacturing jobs for their members, because there will be fewer new cars being built," suggested Claire. "Jane read about that the other day in the paper. Let's call that idea number two."

"Good, and for a third idea, as I mentioned yesterday, the oil and gas manufacturers and retailers would see reduced sales, so they would resist the movement.

"And the body shops and towing companies provide a fourth example," continued Joe. "They would see reduced business, because people driving the speed limit would be less likely to have accidents than if they were speeding."

"Excellent!" Jane said. "Let me get these down. This is great!"

"And police forces could be reduced in size," she suggested, as she had caught up with her note taking, "because there would be fewer speeding violations to chase down. How's that, for a fifth example?"

"Yes, it's good," replied Joe. "Indeed, all organizations that depend on speeders would see a lessening of their role. So we could see resistance from legal systems, due to fewer clients who challenge speeding tickets, including all the infrastructure such as judges, court clerks, and so on. Also road repair crews would have fewer roads to repair, because slower vehicles would cause less damage."

"Wow! And how about tire manufacturers, who would sell fewer tires, because slower driving would allow tires to last longer?" Claire was excited. "Hold on, let's let Jane write these down. What's that, now? We have eight examples."

Joe was also excited. He would not have thought that they could come up with so many examples of organizations that would be inclined to resist the L-movement.

By now they were well into their meals, and they grabbed bits of food among their enthusiastic interactions.

"And do you know what?" Joe asked. "We've only considered organizations that have to do with cars driving the speed limit. Let's think of all the others. Let's call them the spin-off issues, or the ancillary effects, such as the counsellors and psychiatrists who would have less business because people have become more relaxed and at peace with themselves through slowing down."

"Right on!" declared Jane. "That's idea number nine."

"And number ten," she continued, "could be the whole health care system, ironically, with all its infrastructure of hospital emergency rooms, ambulance drivers, drug manufacturers, and all the rest, because more relaxed people would put less of a load on the system." She was proud of picking up that new word "infrastructure," and using it so soon. She was in a groove now, all nervousness gone, but feeling excited as she saw her project coming together.

"Excellent example!" Claire interjected, between bites of her lunch. "Just a moment, I was thinking of ... Oh! Yes! How about television, movie, and other such entertainment producers, who would have to move up a notch in artistic value, because more relaxed consumers would be less interested in lower-level productions. They would demand something more stimulating, more challenging of the intellect. That would put second-rate actors, screenwriters, and so on, out of work."

Joe was not so enthusiastic about that one. "Well, that one may be a bit of a stretch, but let's keep it, anyway. There may not be as big an effect in that industry as for some of the other examples we've come up with."

Drive the self-limits

"Yeah, I think I agree with Joe," declared Jane.

"OK, I'll grant you that," Claire admitted that not all of the ideas would be acceptable in a brainstorming session. "But here's one, from our own personal experience. Families would become more inner-focused, spending more time together, because they were taking time to smell the roses. That's what has happened in our own family. Right, Jane? Now that would have an impact on the whole set of industries that have come to depend on families not spending time together. So, we could see resistance from the sports stadiums, golf and country clubs, liquor stores, and many others, all of whom would see a drop in business. Maybe even video games and other such distractions would become less popular."

"Good one," said Jane. "And how about truck drivers? They will be glad, on one hand, that car drivers will cause them less stress by driving more sensibly, not zipping in and out, cutting them off; but, on the other hand, they will be annoyed by all those slow-moving vehicles blocking them on the roads. And they won't want to slow down, because it's their business to deliver their loads rapidly. This group is a very large and influential one. We just learned in school that the most common job for men in Canada is truck driving."

Why Are Gas Prices So High?

"Really? I didn't know that," replied her mother.

"That's a great one," offered Joe. "So now we have, what's that, say, more than a dozen distinct examples of society's established institutions that will feel the effect of a huge number of people driving the speed limit. They will all have a tendency to resist the movement. And many of our examples can be broken down to sub-groups, such as the many special-interest groups that make up the huge health-care infrastructure."

"This has been great, you guys!" Jane was delighted. "I can't wait to build this list into a report."

"Of course, you'll have to do some research for each group," cautioned Joe. "It will add some validity to each example if you can quote from a newspaper or somewhere a real situation that supports that example."

"Good point, and it would make it a better report to have some real data, rather than just our guesses about how society would respond to the movement. Thanks. And thanks especially for this brainstorming session." Jane was squirming now, anxious to get on with her project.

- - -

Drive the self-limits

Claire was delighted with the results of their meeting.

She was so very proud of Jane that she felt as if she would burst! After dropping Jane off at school, she felt like flowing again, although she was too excited to do so. So she just drove along and thought about things.

"How did Jane become so advanced and so smart?" wondered Claire. "She's still so young! It must have been from Peter's genes, not mine. Yes, we must have done something right."

Claire had never thought of herself as special. She was down to earth, not complicated. She took pleasure in simple things, such as her gardening and her bridge club. Her job was not demanding, but satisfying. Gardening let her get her hands dirty, and bridge kept her mind alert and kept her connected socially with friends.

But this new attention that she was getting was a puzzle to her. Why did everyone credit her with the speed limit idea? Anybody could have thought of that idea. She really did not want the credit, or the fame, or the spotlight. She wanted simply to live her happy family life, raising the girls, being the best wife she could be for Peter, and making some modest contributions on her job.

Why Are Gas Prices So High?

Was there a reason for it all? Was she being led along on this path because it was the right path for her? Was this another form of flowing?

Yes, perhaps that was the explanation. After all, she had meditated for a long time on a clean world, with a peaceful humanity. Why was she resisting? Isn't this an answer to her prayers and her visualizations? Hadn't she brought this solution onto herself and into the world? She had long believed that God works in wondrous ways, and she had told others of her belief, especially her family. But look what was happening—a wondrous way was now working in her own life! And she was resisting it!

Claire had accused Peter and Joe of being too academic. But here she was, herself, being too academic. "Maybe God works in wondrous ways for other people," she thought to herself, "but surely not for Me! I'm above that! Yes, I can meditate on a clean world, but I certainly didn't expect to change my own life, or for messages to come to me—other people, maybe, but not me!" She felt a bit like the teacher who lived the ethic, "Do as I say, not as I do!"

What an elitist attitude! she thought. Was she elitist? Did she consider herself better than others? Well, no ... but also ... yes. She didn't *want* to consider herself better than others, but perhaps she did, a bit. Is it *better* that she felt? Superior? More righteous? No ... not better, but maybe— what was it that she had read about recently?—more advanced ... no ... more *evolved*? Yes, that was it. More evolved, more spiritually evolved. She must have done some good things in previous lives to let her be born into this life at a higher level of evolution. That's what she had read. Evolution does not stop with physical evolution of apes into humans. It continues on, spiritually. And here she was, realizing that she was part of it. Not through academic detachment, pondering and studying evolution, but truly living it, with all its messy details: making the daily choices, the immense number of minute decisions.

My God! What have I done in the last year? Claire felt a distressful panic. *What have I accomplished?* She realized a year ago that she had been given a special mission to spread the word about slowing down to drive the speed limit. And the word really did spread. *But what have I accomplished? Sure, I talked to a few people, gave a few interviews, helped the girls with some schoolwork, cooked lots of meals, washed lots of laundry, planted a few flowers, ... but what of any significance?*

Why Are Gas Prices So High?

Am I drifting into my old ways again? Claire felt ashamed. She was evolved beyond the level of laziness or neglect. But for the past year she had become so bogged down in the trivia of daily life that she had lost sight of the incredible gift that she had been given. For sure, her prayers had been answered, but she had dropped the ball.

"So, what's to be done about it?" Claire asked herself. There's no stopping the movement now, or changing it. Besides, she wouldn't want to stop it, or to change it.

Perhaps she could help the movement along now simply by continuing to speak about it to others, to encourage them, and to offer her own example. And she could continue to meditate on a clean world and to follow her intuition. Yes! She couldn't sit back now and just leave this new movement to its own life.

CHAPTER 9 — *A life of its own*

"Do you think she'll be nice, Mom?"

Mary was curious, and a bit worried, about her mother's upcoming interview with the newspaper reporter.

"Oh, I'm sure the lunch will go well, Honey. I plan to enjoy it," Claire replied, reassuring Mary, hoping that her nervousness was not evident.

Rebecca McGill's reputation preceded her. She was known to be delightfully friendly across the table during an interview, but piercingly brutal with her written stories afterwards. Many of her "Lunch guests" had come to regret their chance remarks, or their uncoordinated wardrobes, or their unconscious habits of twirling their rings or sticking their tongues out.

All of this history Claire carried in her mind in the days leading up to the interview. Rebecca had phoned her a week ago and suggested a lunch meeting. Pleased to be asked, Claire accepted immediately, and then started worrying.

"I'm surprised the car is late," she said. "She sounded so efficient and well organized."

A moment later it rounded the corner and pulled up into her driveway—a sleek, black, official looking car, chauffeur driven, not as ostentations as a limousine, but fancier than an ordinary taxi. After kissing Mary good-bye, Claire's first mistake was to walk out her front door and over to the driveway, before Rebecca had fully emerged from the back seat. That incident would be reported in Rebecca's column the next day as:

> And there she was! All gangly and teenagerly, overly anxious to please. (Was she insecure? Make mental note to look for other indicators.) Claire Atwater bounded down the path like some youngster on her first date. Could this be the

A life of its own

Mother of the L-movement, in a rush to meet me, bubbling over with nervousness, quite the antithesis of inner peacenik? Oh, well! Mustn't let first impressions turn me off!

Claire, lamb being led to slaughter, had no idea what was going on. For some reason, she left her intuition in bed that day.

The drive downtown was filled with small talk, the most dangerous kind, Claire knew, but how could such a charming lady as Rebecca mean any harm? After all, hadn't she flown down from Toronto specifically to see her?

Cute little town. City, actually, but still wet from the paint. Trying to grow up. Claire's daughter and cat pressing their noses to the window, curtains moving on her street, people flashing the L-sign, slow traffic (car ... car ... another car ...), people standing on corners, talking. Hey! Maybe I could like this pace of life. (Joke!)

The restaurant was elegant, and the staff were attentive. Claire noticed their cautiousness in Rebecca's presence. They must have been tipped about the interview with their local hero, and the need for sophistication.

95

Why Are Gas Prices So High?

"So, I hear that your intuition prompted you to start the L-movement." Rebecca took out her notepad to signal the start of the real interview.

Claire had five objections to that opening statement. She did not like this reporter's prying into her personal life, she resented being thought of as the founder of some movement, she was proud of her intuitive sense and felt it was being belittled, and two other objections that she tried later to recall but forgot, scrambling as she was to maintain her composure and to respond professionally.

"Well, uh, ... not really—but, well, yes, I guess so."

The Founder of the L-movement, Saviour of the World, Patron Saint of Civility, fumbled her words, groping for an explanation of how she started it all. She must have left her famous intuition at home today. Why else would she wear white and order tomato minestrone soup?

"But I don't want anyone to call me the founder of a movement," Claire continued. "The idea to slow down and drive the speed limit occurred to me just by chance one day during lunch with a colleague, Joe Carboni. If anything, he should be the founder, because he grabbed the suggestion so enthusiastically and ran with it. No, I didn't

A life of its own

start the L-movement—all I will admit to is perhaps being there when it started."

Her modesty screamed out purity and virginity through the reddish-orange of the minestrone soup. Yes, perhaps a white blouse was correct, after all.

Rebecca guided her on, prompting her with, "Who initiated the 'L-sign' with the fingers?"

Claire was ready for that one. "I honestly don't know. Our daughters say that it used to mean 'Loser,' but for some reason the teenagers just spontaneously switched it over to mean 'Limits,' and it became a greeting and encouragement, rather than an insult. I imagine that the time was right—for many years young people had been active in the ecological awareness area, and they pressed for the earth's sustainable development, so the idea to use less gas came along at a perfect time to be adopted."

"Did you think that it would catch on and spread so quickly?" asked Rebecca, juggling her pen, notepad, fork, napkin, and drink.

"No ... it totally caught us by surprise," Claire replied. "Again, I guess the time was right. People all over the world were ready for some way that they could contribute."

Why Are Gas Prices So High?

"Tell me about your family," asked Rebecca, casually, but watching intently for a reaction.

Damn! Claire wanted to protect the girls and Peter from the limelight. The idea flashed through her mind to decline answering that one. But then she realized that her family life was public knowledge by now, anyway. Magazines, newspapers, television—they had all had a run at trying to sensationalize Claire's private life.

Trying not to skip a heartbeat or spill a drop, Claire nonchalantly offered, "As you're likely aware, my husband, Peter, and I have two daughters: Mary, who is 15, in Grade 10, and Jane, who is 17, and in Grade 12. We're a very close family, and do lots of things together. My proudest aspect of our home life is our Sunday evening Family Time, during which we don't answer the phone, but just spend time together, reading, discussing, playing cards, whatever we want."

> *Is she too squeaky-clean, or what? Her family spends Sunday evenings reading, talking, playing cards, and not answering the phone. What's wrong with this picture? (Subtle voice of envy inside this reporter's guilt-ridden psyche, "Why can't I have that?" Make note to try it. Check if editor will fund it.)*

A life of its own

"And do your girls agree with your 'speed limit' ideas?"

"Oh! For sure! They join me sometimes on trips for speaking engagements. And both are working on school projects related to the idea.

"But what really interests me," Claire leaned forward, unconsciously conveying her enthusiasm, subtly moving the focus away from her home life, "is the inner change in peoples' lives—how the financially-motivated, and perhaps clean air-motivated 'driving the speed limit movement' resulted in an inner peacefulness in people and a growing civility in society. The movement has a life of its own now, and it is about far more than just saving some gas."

Waiters waited, and diners dined. All around them the bustle of the restaurant bustled. They talked at length about slowing down, about self-limits, and about taking responsibility for the world. Rebecca had not expected to be so enthralled by this small-town girl.

Speaking of inner change, Rebecca's brashness had softened. She retained her earlier remarks, but closed in a way that showed through her example that anyone can change, even herself:

Why Are Gas Prices So High?

Dear Reader: I wish you had been here. I wish you could have met this charming lady in real life, and not merely through my words.

Claire grew up in a small town, met Peter at university, and they settled here in this city to work and raise their family. Nothing spectacular happened in their lives until that fateful day when Claire had her now famous lunch with Joe Carboni.

But if you could have been with us as we talked, I believe that you would have been captivated by this woman, as I was.

Her self-effacing modesty is straight from a Victorian novel. Her genuineness is extremely refreshing. Her candor and simplicity make me wish that I could live here and be friends with her.

I'm glad that I resisted my earlier skepticism and cynicism, and obeyed my editor's direction to fly here and interview Claire. My strong advice to you, dear reader, is to watch for opportunities to hear Claire Atwater giving a talk somewhere.

Attend it!

And I hope, when you hear her story, that it will make a fundamental change in your life.

CHAPTER 10 — *Reactions to the L-movement*

Jane was standing in front of her Grade 12 Science class, presenting her report, motivated and proud. She had titled it "Reactions to Social Change: Newton's Third Law Applied to the L-Movement."

She had introduced her hypothesis that Newton's Third Law applied not only to physical bodies, but also to social systems. She had described the beneficial aspects of the L-movement, having explained that her project would focus on its effect on society. She then moved to the third part of her talk.

Why Are Gas Prices So High?

"Now that I have explained my hypothesis and introduced the L-movement as the major example of a social system for my study, let me now illustrate the hypothesis by giving some examples of 'equal and opposite reactions' to the actions of the L-movement."

Jane's nervousness had vanished. Getting started was what she needed. Besides, why should she be nervous—how many times had she rehearsed this speech and improved it? It was even a bit fun, talking without notes, just using the prompts of the bullet points on her overhead slides.

"I should state at the outset that I have found many reactions that are 'opposite' to the L-movement's actions, but at this point I am not able to measure whether they are 'equal' to those actions.

"This table summarizes some thirteen reactions to the L-movement by various interest groups." Jane projected on the screen her table that summarized the brainstorming that she and her mother had done with Joe.

"I don't have time in this presentation to describe each of the groups—the written report treats them all in some detail—but I will elaborate on just the three that are highlighted. I've chosen one from each category. First, actions that are 'Direct,' meaning that the L-movement has a direct effect on a group, such as a financial impact, or an impact on employment levels.

"Secondly, 'Indirect' actions, which are secondary, or spin-off, ones, such as an impact on quality of life, or on life support professions such as doctors, and so on. And thirdly, actions that have a mixture of direct and indirect effects, such as the legal system."

TABLE 1. Reactions by Groups to the L-Movement Action on Speed Limits

	Group	Type of Action	Reason for Reaction	Description of Reaction
1	Car manufacturers	Direct	Cars will last longer by slower driving, so fewer cars will be sold	Resistance, advertising pressure for faster driving
2	Manufacturing unions	Direct	Manufacturing jobs will be reduced in number	Protests, alliances with management
3	Oil & gas producers and retailers	Direct	Reduced sales, because of reduced consumption	Lower prices, then advertising pressure for the good life of consumption
4	Body shops & tow companies	Direct	Reduced business, due to fewer accidents	Lobbying and funding of a return to the old days
5	Police forces	Direct	Fewer speeding violations would need fewer officers to police	Possible overreaction in other areas
6	Legal/judicial system	Direct & indirect	Fewer challenges of speeding violations would reduce staff needed to prosecute	Discontent among clerks and infrastructure
7	Road repair crews	Direct	Slower vehicles would cause less road damage, so fewer workers	Possible slowdown in work, to stretch out jobs
8	Tire manufacturers	Direct	Slower driving would let tires last longer	(as for #1)

TABLE 1. Reactions by Groups to the L-Movement Action on Speed Limits

	Group	Type of Action	Reason for Reaction	Description of Reaction
9	Counselling professionals	Direct & indirect	More relaxed people would need less counselling	Tendency to prolong unrelated counselling
10	Health care infrastructure	Indirect	More relaxed people would need less hospitalization, fewer drugs	Labour unrest
11	Entertainment producers	Indirect	More relaxed people would want higher cultural levels in entertainment, reducing need for second-rate artists	Labour unrest in the entertainment industry
12	Sports and recreation organizations	Indirect	Business would drop as people became more family oriented	Unemployed people would increase strain on social system
13	Truck drivers	Direct	Slow drivers would interfere with their work.	Increased road rage, political pressure to accommodate truckers

"So, let me start with a Direct example," Jane continued. "The most obvious one is number three, the oil and gas companies. They will resist the L-movement because they will see decreased revenues due to the less

Why Are Gas Prices So High?

gas consumption by a large number of people driving more slowly than beforehand. In fact, it turns out that reducing speed 18% from 110 to 90 kilometres per hour can reduce gas consumption by up to 25%.

"This next chart is from our local newspaper, about a month ago. It plots global oil production, in billions of barrels per year. You can see that last year had the first dip in growth in at least twenty years, peaking at around 27 billions of barrels of oil produced that year. Now, it was not

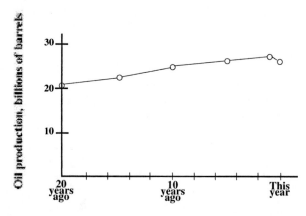

much of a dip, perhaps about 2% from the previous year. And if we looked in more detail, we would see some small dips in other years. This year's decrease may not be totally due to the L-movement's effect, because other energy sources are making their mark, such as hydrogen fuel cells, and because we may be reaching the limit of how much oil there is in the earth. However, at least this recent dip in oil production is encouraging.

"So the petroleum industry has a strong reason to dislike the L-movement and to react negatively to it. Their reaction will likely include trying to persuade people to buy more gas by lowering their prices temporarily, advertising pressure, and other means."

She paused for a moment and looked around the room, to get a sense of whether her classmates were understanding her presentation. She had a momentary flash of panic, realizing how very exposed and alone she was in that room. Why were none of her classmates asking any questions? Why were they just sitting there blankly? Was she that far out to lunch, so extremely isolated from her peers?

But then it flowed. The show must go on. Break a leg.

It was amazing to her how rapidly her mind worked when she was under pressure or in situations of high tension. Some autonomous mechanism seemed to engage, some high-performance system took over. She didn't will it; it simply happened. Her panic gave way to a clarity of mind, a sense of mission, and a serene calmness.

Three reasons for everyone's silence became clear. First, the students were embarrassed to ask any questions. Perhaps they didn't want to embarrass her, or they didn't want to reveal their ignorance, or maybe they were totally flabbergasted by her presentation and they were the ones who were out to lunch or at the beach.

This revelation made her feel compassionate towards her classmates.

The second reason for their silence could be that Jane was more advanced than the others. After all, hadn't she researched her project thoroughly and rehearsed it repeatedly? Didn't she have a considerable advantage over the others by being part of a great family, especially being the daughter of the founder of the L-movement? Yes, she felt as if she were from another planet. Better? No—just different, perhaps more evolved, but not smarter or more advanced. Correct? No—just fortunate to be born into her current circumstances.

Jane felt a humility flowing over her sense of self.

And the third reason that had shown itself to her was her sense of perspective. She realized that she really knew her stuff and that she must slow down. She had researched

Reactions to the L-movement

and pondered and wrote and rehearsed this speech. But these students are now hearing it all for the first time. Her father had coached her during a dry run to slow down, or not to try to explain everything, for the benefit of her audience. Now she had a glimpse of just how right he was.

And she felt a sense of purpose, or mission. She was meant to be here and to do this.

So there, in the heat of the moment, Jane saw with vivid clarity a vision of her cosmic role. Just a flash. All of this in a fraction of a second. Everyone watching.

But the show must go on.

"Now, for a second example to examine," Jane continued, "I'd like to look at number 12, the sports and recreation facilities. This is an Indirect action, having a peripheral, or indirect impact on people and groups.

"As people become more peaceful inwardly, due to slowing down their driving and their lives, they can be expected to become more family oriented. This in turn will lead them to spend more quality time together as a family than formerly. So we can expect to see a reaction from

109

many of the industries that currently benefit from families not spending time together.

"I want to focus on just one of the groups that will have a negative reaction—golf and country clubs. Why do people belong to such clubs? I suggest that it is for a variety of reasons: social, sporting, business, and, for our purposes, the key one, escapism. Yes, I believe that a considerable number of memberships in golf and country clubs can be traced to people wanting to escape from their boring family lives.

"Now, suppose family life could be made less boring. If that were the case, then there would be less incentive to escape from it, and then golf and country clubs would see a drop in membership.

"Well, that's exactly what the L-movement does. People become more inwardly calm and at peace with themselves. They become more accepting of their place in life, and less anxious to resist it or to change it. This attitude extends to those around such people, namely, their families. A warmer, more comfortable family life results, and one's spouse and children become more interesting, more vitalizing, and less boring.

Reactions to the L-movement

"This is a well-understood point in social psychology. It's called the 'Feel good, do good' phenomenon, and it has observed that happy people are helpful people. If people feel good about themselves, they will be more altruistic, more pleasant, and more friendly.

"And so the eventual result is that people who slow down their lives don't feel the need as much to escape from their families, but they are more content with their family lives. It is a simple step from there to a drop in golf and country club memberships.

"Now, the drop may not be very significant. Suppose that only ten percent of such memberships are due to the 'escapist' reason. And suppose that only ten percent of those people withdraw their memberships when they become more inwardly peaceful. So for a club that has 1000 members, ten might drop out. Not a big number. But, when you expand that membership drop to the many other sports and recreation organizations that might be similarly affected, we are talking of a significant number of people. Thus, we could see drops in participation at bowling lanes, spectator sports such as baseball, football, and hockey, yacht clubs, social drinking bars, video gaming stores, and other places.

"Thus, the many sports and recreation organizations will have reason to dislike the L-movement, and to react to it, say by means of advertising and incentives to recruit new members or retain current ones. They will also increase their drive to attract families, and they may develop special programs for them."

Jane paused again to see if her fellow students were following her train of thought, or if they had any questions or comments.

"Do you have any data to back up your claims?" one of the students asked.

Ah! Some interaction. Her internal dialogue must have helped a bit, creating some attunement with her classmates. Jane's features softened just a tiny amount, and she leaned forward slightly.

She had to admit that much of her research was abstract, not based on evidence, "Well, apart from the 'Feel good, do good' behaviour that I mentioned, I can't claim that my predictions are based on measured data. However, I don't think that makes the research less valid, but simply that it is based on sound reasoning, I hope, and that it forms a hypothesis suggesting that further research is needed."

Seeing a few heads nodding and some smiles of agreement, she continued. "And for my final example, let us look at number nine, the counselling professions. This is a mixture of Direct and Indirect actions.

"As people slow down their lives and become more relaxed and at peace with themselves, we can expect that they will depend less on those professions that offer help to people under stress. Thus, we can expect less business for counsellors, psychiatrists, social workers, and so on.

"Let's focus on just counsellors. There are all sorts of counsellors: family counsellors, individual counsellors, Jungian analysts, spiritual directors, financial coaches, and so on. All of them would feel a lessening of their business if people had less stress and anxiety in their lives.

"Now, that drop in business could encourage counsellors to make up for it through other means, such as prolonging their sessions with other clients, lowering their threshold for accepting new clients, making people feel the need for counselling, and other means. After all, nobody likes to see his or her business drop, so they will resist forces that tend to draw people away from them.

"And when we add in with counsellors others in the caring professions, including psychiatrists, psychoanalysts, the clergy, social workers, psychologists, and so on, we can see that the L-movement has an effect across the business of many such professionals.

"So, we can expect that these caring professionals will have reason to resist the actions of the L-movement."

"Now I must wrap up this presentation. It is important to reiterate that I have not even addressed part of my hypothesis, that in social systems such as the L-movement there is for every action an *equal* and *opposite* reaction. I have not addressed the *equal* part. I don't know how to measure the force or intensity of a social action or reaction. But I do feel confident that I have identified a variety of *opposite* reactions to the L-movement, although I cannot say whether they are equal or not.

"I would expect that such measurements would be a good subject for a university research project, and I hope to do such research in my own university studies, starting this Fall. Similarly, another area for research, I believe, is in personal reactions to inner change. It would be very interesting to observe the mental and psychic reactions that occur when one forces a change in one's inner life, such as trying to break a long-standing habit, or trying to change a pessimistic attitude into an optimistic one.

"I hope that it is clear from my presentation that, using the L-movement as an example, there can be many opposite reactions to an action upon a social system. We have examined three of them in this study, the reactions that come from oil and gas companies, from sports and recreation facilities, and from the counselling professions.

"I believe that this project has demonstrated support for my hypothesis that Newton's Third Law applies not only to physical systems, but also to social systems, in other words, for every social action there are—possibly equal and—opposite reactions.

"Thank you for the opportunity to present my findings to you. I would be pleased to make the printed report available to anyone who is interested."

*Part C: **One Year Ago***

CHAPTER 11 — *Why drive the speed limit?*

"OK, folks. I can't hold back any longer."

Luke Brookside was starting to soften a bit, admitting that it was not just a passing fad.

"We'll devote the first hour of the show to that ... what's its name-movement? Oh, yeah! The L-movement. All right! Yes, I know full well what its name is. I'm just being my usual smart-assed self. After all—you've come to expect it of me, haven't you?"

Then he lowered his voice. "But, seriously, folks ... before I take the first call, I have something important to

Why Are Gas Prices So High?

say. I have a confession to make! I never thought I'd admit this ... but ... well, you're not gonna believe it—and I don't want you spreading the word—but, I drove the speed limit yesterday!

"There—I've said it! Hello, my name is Luke, and I'm a speed limit driver!"

His voice became even more sober and quiet. "Actually, I'm really serious here, folks. I thought I'd give it a try. What's this—more than two years since I've heard about the L-movement? So, well, maybe there's something to it. Maybe I'm ready to listen to what you have to say about it.

"So let's take the first caller. Good morning, Cindy. You're on the air."

"Hello, Luke. Thank you for that confession. I'm glad you're trying it."

"No promises, Cindy," Luke interrupted. "But let nobody claim that good, old Luke is a bigot!"

Cindy decided not to touch that one. She asked, "May I explain why I drive the speed limit?"

Luke replied, sort of semi-reluctantly, "OK! Go ahead."

Why drive the speed limit?

"Well, I want to save the earth's resources and its health not just for my children and grandchildren, which is the usual reason that people give. My interest is for them, yes, but also because I'll be back, too, and I want the earth and all its people to be in good shape."

Luke couldn't hold back his question, "What do you mean, you'll be back?"

"Yes. We'll all be back. In another life. You see, reincarnation and karma are facts of life."

"Sorry, Cindy. Tilt! I can't permit religious discussions on this program." Luke was ready to switch to the next caller. "We're Canadian, you know!"

Cindy countered with, "I'm not talking religion, Luke. Reincarnation and karma are actual facts. Whether a religious group accepts or rejects those facts is not relevant and makes no difference to the reality. The truth remains, whether you believe it or not. The truth is that I'll be back and I'll be compensated for my thoughts and actions. That motivates me to drive the speed limit. Indeed, my previous thoughts and actions have partly created the world as it is now, and I want to create a better world for the future."

Why Are Gas Prices So High?

Luke had heard enough. "All right, thank you for your call, Cindy. We have to move on now.

"Well, folks, I get some real weirdos calling. I guess that's my 'karma,' huh?" Luke snickered. "So, next we have David. Good morning, David."

"Good morning, Luke. Your previous caller was correct. We must recognize the long-term effects of our present way of life."

"Oh, No! Not another nut case!" Luke sighed in exasperation.

"Call me what you like, Luke," David responded. "But there are far more people out here than you may realize, who conduct their lives respecting the law of karma. You see, driving the speed limit is a spiritual practice for us, not merely a way of saving gas."

"Well La-Di-Da!" sneered Luke. "I confine my spiritual practices to church services."

"The real service starts when the church service ends," countered David.

Why drive the speed limit?

"Ah! Good one! OK—I stand corrected, David. Thank you for your call."

David caught him in time. "May I add one more thing?"

"Oh, sorry, David. Yes, go ahead."

"Thanks. I just wanted to explain that what we're talking about here is like a sacrament. Do you know what a sacrament is, Luke?"

"Well, how about you, David? Do you know what a phone cut-off switch is?"

David continued, ignoring Luke's sarcasm, "The key point about a sacrament is that it is an inner transformation that has some outer sign which is symbolic of it. So, for the sacrament of baptism, for example, the inner change is a spiritual rebirth, and the outer symbol is immersion in, or signing with, water."

"OK, most people know that. So what's your point, David?"

"Well, a similar situation exists with the L-movement, Luke. Externally, we see people driving the speed limit.

But the really important change is the inner transformation in people as they slow down their lives and become more peaceful and serene.

"You see, it's the sacramental nature of the L-movement that explains why it has the power to catch on and spread so rapidly. It has a very powerful spiritual energy. Powerful enough to resist, or I should say, to rise above the huge amount of negative reaction that resists the positive energy of the L-movement. Have you any idea, Luke, how many people don't want the L-movement to succeed? There's a huge number of people who want current conditions to stay just as they are."

Luke interrupted him with, "That's all very interesting, David, but I think your speech belongs on some other talk show."

"That may be the case, but just one final thought, if I may," replied David. "You see, many of us who feel energized by the L-movement acknowledge that people in the developing countries will want to drive fast, and to have their turn with big cars and comfortable lifestyles. After all, we in the developed world have had our chance, and we are the envy of many others. Now we must step back and let them have their turn. It's sort of an extension of what your

Why drive the speed limit?

previous caller was saying ... We are All One! What we must do here is to lower our expectations a bit, and help the others realize their dreams and get through it as smoothly as possible, so that all of civilization can reach a comfortable level, living peacefully in a sustainable world."

Luke interjected, "So what you're saying, David, is that you want us to cut back from two cars per family to one, to give one car to someone in the developing world, and then lay back while they leapfrog over us."

"You exaggerate, as usual, Luke. What I'm saying is that we are all One. It would be morally wrong for us to deny our brothers and sisters the lifestyle that we have enjoyed. Just like there is individual karma, there is also collective karma and national karma. What we as a country do now, and what we as a developed world do now will influence our future condition. If I flaunt my good fortune of being born into the relative luxury of a well-off Canadian family, then I must accept the strong likelihood that I will be born in a later life in less desirable circumstances, or with a severe sickness, or in an underdeveloped country, as compensation. Similarly, if Canada ignores ..."

"You guys really believe that stuff, don't you?" Luke interrupted. He wanted to explore David's ideas a bit, rather than hanging up as he normally would have done.

"Well, it's more than believing, Luke, but actually *knowing* that these things are true." David was calm and self-assured.

Luke poked him with, "And how do you *know*, for example, that you will come back in an underdeveloped country? For that matter, if you know so much, do you know that I'm going to cut you off any moment now? Is that your karma?"

"Don't be trite, Luke," replied David. "You don't hear me belittling your viewpoints, do you? Let me respond to your main question. As for future lives, I have no idea which specific body I will be born into or which country I will live in. But I do know that my present actions will influence my future conditions in a way that compensates for them—both positively and negatively—sort of like what Newton said about actions resulting in reactions, but on a much bigger, cosmic scale.

"As for how I know about the reality of karma, the law of compensation, as opposed to just believing in it, that's

Why drive the speed limit?

hard to say. Let me try to illustrate by an example. Do you love your wife, Luke?"

"Well, of course I do," snarled Luke, indignantly.

"No, Luke, what I mean is do you *really* love your wife. I don't want just a snap answer, but I'd like you to pause, think for a moment, and tell me whether you love your wife."

Without the slightest pause, Luke growled back, "Look, David, when I say something I mean it. I don't need to pause and think—yes, I do love my wife."

"How do you know, Luke?"

"What do you mean, how do I ...." Luke stopped. This time he paused. "OK, David, you got me. You're asking me whether I *believe* I love my wife or *know* it."

"And which is it, Luke?"

"But knowing I love my wife is far different than knowing I'll be back in another life."

"Is it?" David prodded gently.

"Yes it is. And this conversation's going nowhere. I have lots of other people waiting to talk."

"Luke, the best service you can do for your listeners right now is to stay with this conversation another minute or so."

"I don't think those people on hold would agree with you."

"I disagree!" David risked a cut-off. "My bet is that at least half of them are very interested in this conversation, and they want to hear more. Just let me add one point, and then I'll say good-bye.

"My point is that just as you know you love your wife, and just as you know that deep inside, you are uniquely and specifically you, Luke, in just the same way you can know, with certain knowledge, many things about your role in the Grand Scheme of things. If you don't think that you have that knowledge readily accessible, then a simple discipline of meditation for some time, properly focused, will bring that knowledge to your consciousness.

"And it's that assurance of our cosmic role that inspires us about the beauty of the L-movement: adopting a small cutback in our standard of living results in a huge increase in our inner development and our evolution as a species and as a planet."

CHAPTER 12   *Creating the future*

"So, how does your intuition work, Claire?"

Joe and Claire had not met for lunch for seven months. Their lives had become much busier since the L-movement had caught on, ironically. The original advocates of slowing down had actually sped up. They had drifted further apart, seeing each other less often. And yet, in some ways they were closer together. Their conversations were fewer now, but deeper. They cut through the trivia and straight to the significant topics. It was like some unwritten, mutually understood rule with them that their times together were precious, and they didn't want to waste any moments.

Why Are Gas Prices So High?

They had just ordered their meals. Claire had no hesitation in replying, "My intuition? I would expect it works the same way as yours does!"

"Ha!" Joe laughed. "My intuition is distinguished by its non-existence."

"Not so," she countered. "It's there. You may not be using it regularly, but for sure you have it."

"But yours is the one that's famous. Tell me how it works."

"How it works. Well, I probably can't give you a technical explanation of the physical or psychic laws governing the operation of the human intuitive faculty," said Claire, aware of the role reversal, in which she now seemed to be playing Joe's usual academic part, "but I could describe what intuition does for me and what I do to listen for it."

"Good," replied Joe. "That's a good start."

Claire thought for a moment, and then started. "Well, my intuition is like a little voice that urges me very subtly to do something, like turning this way or that, or choosing this thing or that, or to think of some idea, such as slowing down to drive at the speed limit. What I've done over the years is to train myself to listen carefully for that small voice. And, of course, it's not a real voice, like a person talking inside my head saying things like, 'Turn left here!' but a subtle, distinct urge to turn left. It's not a command, but more like a feeling that I've learned to be attentive to."

Joe was intrigued, "So how did you train yourself?"

"Oh, I forget how it started—perhaps when I read Richard Bucke's book *Cosmic Consciousness* in university—yes, I think that book was the first to influence my evolution to awaken my intuitive sense. And over the years I sort of developed a technique that seems to work for me."

Their meals arrived, and they poked a bit at them. But Joe and Claire were more interested in the non-physical nourishment that they got from their conversation.

Claire took Joe's raised eyebrows as an invitation to continue. "I think the best way to explain the technique is to describe how I create the future."

"Create the future?" asked Joe.

"Yeah. Let me tell you about how I find things that are lost. Last year I was visiting my father for a few days, and he asked me to help him find something that he had misplaced. It was a service award pin that he had received from one of his clubs, for the 40th anniversary of his membership. He hadn't seen the pin for a couple of years, and could not figure out what had happened to it. Part of the trouble was that he couldn't remember whether the pin was in a big package or a small one, flat or round, brown envelope or white. And ever since Mom died, his memory has been failing, so I didn't have much to go on for my searching.

"So I looked in all the obvious places, including all his closets, drawers, boxes, and shelves. I even looked on the lapels and in the pockets of his suits, in the hope that he had worn the pin on some occasion. After searching for a couple of sessions, perhaps three hours total, I was ready to give up.

"Then I decided to create a future in which I had found the pin. I went to a quiet room, cleared my mind, and visualized, as clearly as I could, in as much detail as I could, my hands holding the pin. Now, since I didn't know what the pin looked like—gold or silver, round or square—I couldn't visualize an actual picture of the pin in my hands. But I could imagine what feeling I would have when I found it: a feeling of joy and elation. So I tried my best to

Creating the future

visualize that future state of feeling thrilled by having found Dad's pin.

"Then, when I had painted a very clear image in my mind of what I wanted the future to look and feel like, I released the image, and spoke quietly the words, 'If it is God's will, it is *done*!' I then thanked God for making it happen, and forgot about looking for the pin. I allowed myself to be fully confident that the future would be just as I had visualized. I had no doubts and no worries about it."

"Fascinating!" exclaimed Joe.

Claire continued, "So I went about that evening, doing various things, enjoying my visit with Dad, but not even thinking about the pin. That was to be my last night of the visit. The next day, around noon, I was scheduled to return home.

"As I woke up, or perhaps it was sometime in the night, the idea occurred to me to ask Dad whether he wanted to write a note to enclose with a gift that he was sending back with me for Peter, my husband. Over breakfast, Dad liked the idea of writing a note. I offered to get some note paper for him, and he told me that he thought there might be some blank cards with envelopes in the bottom left drawer of a desk. I went to look there and found a stack of miscellaneous papers and large brown envelopes. I flipped through the stack, looking for notecards, finding none, but at the very bottom I found two large envelopes. I pulled them out.

"Would you believe that one of those envelopes contained Dad's pin that he had lost?

"The pin was enclosed in a leather wallet, likely the original presentation package, which was inside a long box, which in turn was inside the envelope! As I pulled out the pin, I held it in my hands and felt the same excitement that I had visualized the previous evening!"

"Amazing!" whistled Joe.

"In the previous two days I had seen that envelope a couple of times in my searching, but had ignored it because it didn't fit with my mental image of the pin that I was looking for.

"However, my intuition urged me to search for something else, not the pin. Indeed, the whole scenario of needing notepaper may have been fabricated, likely by my own unconscious, specifically to make me search in that drawer and to open envelopes to see if there was any notepaper inside."

Joe was impressed. "That's a wonderful story!" he said. "Is it true?"

"Yes," Claire responded.

"So what you're saying is that you created a future state that you wanted in your mind, and in order for it to become real, something, which you call your intuition, urged you to do some quite unrelated task, which led you to the very future state you wanted."

"Exactly! Apart from some details, you've got it right. And that's only one example. I've found a great many lost objects by that method, and influenced a great many things to happen."

"Very intriguing!" Joe pondered the vast implications of this method for a moment. "So is that the method you used to found the L-movement—or I mean, to come up with the idea of driving the speed limit?"

"Yes, essentially a similar process. For a long time I had been trying to create a future in which there was less atmospheric pollution, by visualizing the earth with clean

Why Are Gas Prices So High?

air all around it. Sometimes I need to have many visualization attempts before I get results, and I probably visualized a clean earth once per week for many months. The key thing seems to be making the mental image clear, in great detail, and also releasing the image with gratitude and with no doubts that the future state will occur. And then I have to be open to my intuitive urges, and just flow with them. So in this case, I had a distinct urge to mention the speed limit idea to you that day at lunch."

"So the answers come to you from your intuition," observed Joe.

"Well ... I think I'd rather call it guidance than answers," Claire replied. "If I wait for the answer to a specific question, I'll likely not get it. But if I remain open for general inspiration, it always comes.

"The key thing is to trust my intuition. I have to listen for that subtle, intuitive voice or urging, and to follow its guidance, even though the guidance may seem silly or irrelevant. So, for example, if I had been looking for Dad's pin, I would have ignored any inner voice that suggested looking in the bottom left drawer, because I had checked that drawer twice already. It was important that I stop searching for the pin, because I had already created a future in which I have found the pin. Instead, I had to listen to my intuition, which urged me to ask Dad whether he wanted to write a note.

"Similarly, it was important that I stop looking for ways to fix the earth's atmosphere, because I had already created a future in which the earth has a clean atmosphere. I had to be open to my intuition, and I did receive the urge to mention driving the speed limit to you.

"And it's vital to express gratitude again when the whole process works. If I don't acknowledge the source of my intuition, then I can't expect to appeal to it again."

"Wow! That's a very powerful technique!" Joe had not realized anything about this spiritual aspect of Claire's life. "Properly applied, it could change the world. Especially if people coordinated their efforts."

"Yes, that's exactly what it's all about, Joe. Changing one's own little world by visualizing, dismissing the image with confidence, listening to one's intuition, and then following its guidance, with gratitude. I'm thinking of teaching the technique to others, to amplify our individual efforts. A set of small changes can lead to a huge change."

"So how does your intuition know just what advice to give you?" asked Joe.

"Now that I don't know," admitted Claire. "I believe that the intuitive faculty taps into a higher source that sees the big picture, and can think outside the box, to give advice that our limited, rational minds would not even conceive."

"So it's a form of prayer," Joe observed.

"Yes, that's right. In fact, often I just call it that. I'll tell someone that I pray about finding something lost, if I don't want to get into a long explanation. But it's not traditional prayer in which one appeals to a deity for intervention. It's more the application of certain laws of the universe, like intuition tapping into a higher source, or like creating the future by visualizing it. I call it co-creating the world along with the higher powers of the universe.

"I would guess that traditional prayer works in a similar way, but the person who is praying expects God to do the work, through various forms of miracles. I expect me to do the work, through principles that are becoming well-understood as our human species evolves."

Creating the future

"Could you give me an example?" asked Joe.

"Well, OK," Claire thought for a moment, and then continued. "Traditional prayer might take the form of, 'Dear God: Please make Joe better,' as a supplication when Joe is sick. The co-creating method involves visualizing Joe in good health, releasing that image with confidence that it has come to be, and then listening carefully for the intuitive urge that will prompt me for my role in helping Joe achieve good health. And then I must act on what my intuition advises me to do. For example, I may have to allow the healing, creative powers to flow through me to Joe, or I may need to phone or visit him to encourage him, or I may need to mention him to a friend who may be inspired with some idea for helping Joe to get better. And finally I express gratitude for the opportunity to serve in this way."

"So co-creating the world, as you call it, involves a lot of participation, rather than just praying and forgetting about it."

"Yes, that's right," replied Claire. "It involves taking responsibility, or I like to think of it as a stewardship, for the world, and actively participating in creating the future that I wanted."

141

Why Are Gas Prices So High?

Joe could see how a lot of Claire's ways were explainable, now that he had some insight into her philosophy of creating the future. "No wonder you thought of driving the speed limit!"

Claire was modest, as usual. "But, something I really want you to understand is that it was not I who thought of driving the speed limit, but my intuition. Or, to be more precise, it was the source of my intuition, what we might call God, or the creative intelligence and Love of the universe, or the cosmic wisdom, and that source communicated the idea to me via my intuition.

"You see, if I had dreamed up the speed limit idea on my own, it would almost certainly have failed to work. The timing might have been wrong, or the location. But the cosmic wisdom of the universe, or God, knows the best time and place and manner. It sees the big picture, as I've mentioned before. And it spoke to me through my intuition at our lunch two years ago, urging me to suggest driving the speed limit as a way to save gas. And it perhaps gave intuitive urges to others, to bring their actions into harmony with mine, in order for the future to flow as I had created it psychically. It knew that the optimum time for that idea was then, and that you, Joe, were the optimum person to mention it to. It knew that humanity was at the optimum point of readiness for the idea."

"Yes, I see," said Joe. "And only a higher source would have anticipated the sacramental nature of the idea. The real value of driving the speed limit is not saving gas, but the inward transformation of people to become more peaceful and content. It's just like you being led astray to look for notepaper in order that you actually find your father's pin."

"So that's why the speed limit movement caught on so quickly and so profoundly, even against such a huge resistance of all the groups that didn't want it to succeed," said Claire. "It is rooted in a cosmic energy that feeds and sustains it. It was meant to be!"

CHAPTER 13   *One*

"Phone for you, Jane!"

Mary knew that Jane did not want to be disturbed. The sign *Don't Bug Me!* on her door made that clear. But the caller was Jane's boyfriend, so it seemed reasonable to ignore the sign.

"Take a message," came muttering in a low, distracted voice through the closed door.

"But it's Ron!" Mary was glad that she had put the call on hold, so that Ron couldn't hear this exchange.

Why Are Gas Prices So High?

Jane was really annoyed now—at Ron for calling, at Mary for disturbing her, and at herself for not being more forceful in explaining how serious she was when she asked not to be bugged. "Please tell him I'll call back," Jane insisted. "And then come in, will you?"

Jane had been meditating. Why had Ron called at this very moment, and why had Mary ignored her sign? There must be a reason. Even that was worth meditating on.

Mary rapped quietly on the door, and opened it a crack. "Sorry," she confessed. "I gave him the message. But I figured that Ron was allowed to interrupt anything. Were you meditating?"

"Yes," Jane responded. "But it's OK, Little Sister, because in the last few seconds I had a beautiful insight about why interruptions occur. Come on in!"

Puzzled, intrigued, and relieved, Mary stepped through the door into her older sister's bedroom. The disarray shouted out for acknowledgment: socks, jeans, books, photos, scattered CD cases, cosmetic bottles and tubes, school projects and supplies, partly opened drawers with clothes hanging out, lingerie dangling from the ceiling fan, shoes here and there. "Where can I walk? Is there a floor?"

One

Welcome to Jane's room. Who would have guessed that such chaos would be occupied by such an orderly, disciplined, intelligent young lady? The contrast was startling! Perhaps this private sanctum was her release from discipline. This was the same Jane whose favourite quote, posted on her wall, was from Francis de Sales:

> *Half an hour's meditation is essential, except when you are busy. Then a full hour is needed.*

"Quick! I want to tell you," beckoned Jane, patting the bed for Mary to sit down. She ignored her questions about how to navigate from the door to the bed. Jane realized how messy her room was. She couldn't help it. That's just how she was.

"OK—so tell me." Mary was mildly awestruck by Jane. She loved her, but she was also puzzled by her. They were close enough in ages that they shared clothes and often did things together. But Mary realized that her sister was different somehow; indeed, her whole family was different. She felt a distinct tug from her peer group to draw away from Jane, as if she were embarrassed to be seen with a nerd, a geek who was different.

Jane knew all this about Mary. And today felt like the right time to talk about it.

"Yes, I was meditating," she began. "And I don't like being disturbed in the middle of a session. But this time I caught my anger and held it back, to quiet my mind for a moment to consider why Ron called at that very moment and why you interrupted me."

"I'm sorry."

"No, really, it's OK. It turned out well. Let me explain.

"As you know from what Mom has told us, everything has a reason—every person, every thing, every event, every phone call, every little sister that interrupts a meditation session."

"Weird!" Mary shivered. "This is spooky!"

"Well, I wouldn't say that," continued Jane. "It's not spooky or weird. It's simply an aspect of reality that we don't understand very well yet. It's simply the universe behaving according to its natural laws—not supernatural, but following the laws of nature—and we human beings are gradually learning about them, or perhaps relearning, as some would say."

One

"I still think it's creepy!"

"I understand. But let me continue.

"You see, I caused Ron to call just now," Jane stated. "And I caused you to answer the phone and to interrupt me. The reason that I caused those events was to teach me a lesson."

Mary was wide-eyed and fully absorbed. "Wow! Spooky, but cool!"

"I don't mean that I used some magical powers to make Ron call me, or to make you interrupt me. What happened was that Ron responded to his intuitive urge to phone me at that moment, and you listened to your intuition to interrupt me.

"And the reason that the two of you received those intuitive urges was that I had been meditating for weeks on how I could improve my self, my whole being, in order to become the very best that I was meant to be. I had visualized many times myself being a highly effective instrument for good in the world.

"So, after I had visualized it clearly, after I had 'created the future' as Mom would say, I then had to slow down regularly and listen very carefully for signs and messages for me, advising me on what to do in order to achieve that future that I had created in my mind."

Mary was fascinated. "Wow! I didn't know that you actually believed all that stuff!"

"Oh, yes, more than believing. Actually practicing it. I know that I'm only a beginner, and I've got a long way to go, but it sure is fun working on my development this way. I feel so very grateful to have been born into this family and to be given such a head start."

"So let me guess ... the interruptions were messages to you?" Mary suggested.

"You got it, Little Sister! That's exactly it. You see, God speaks to us all the time, with guidance and advice, in so many, many ways. A phrase of music here, a chance meeting there, a daydream or night dream, an insight, a mental image, a slip of the tongue ..."

"An interruption."

"Yes, an interruption. Now, ordinarily I consider interruptions to be annoyances. Everyone does, I would expect. But after I have created a future in which I am as effective as I can be, then I had better listen to all inputs as meaningful. And an interruption is an input.

"You see, if my motive is pure, and if I'm striving to help God to co-create the world, then I attract all sorts of constructive, creative energy to me to help me on that path. So, these interruptions form part of that energy."

"But what do they mean?" asked Mary.

"Well, this is the neat part," replied Jane. "I think that I attracted the interruptions to myself to compensate for how self-centered and inward-focused I was becoming. The interruptions are meant to remind me that there are other important people out there, whom I must not ignore, especially because I have created a future in which I am highly effective. In such a future, I can't be inward-focused, but I must be receptive and accommodating to everyone else, and interacting with them. So Ron *had* to call me, in order to help me in a way that he could not have imagined. And you *had* to interrupt me for a similar reason.

"It's Newton's Third Law in action again. I had gone too far in one direction, my pendulum had swung one way, and the reaction in the other direction was to bring me back, eventually to a balanced position."

151

Why Are Gas Prices So High?

"Neat!" Mary was impressed.

"And it's even bigger than that," Jane continued. "You've heard Mom tell us that 'We are all One,' haven't you?"

Mary hesitated a bit. "Yes ... but I never really understood it."

"Same here. But I've been reading about it and meditating on it. I have glimpses into what it means now and then. What I've found is that it is a wonderful explanation for reality, filling in the gaps that are left by modern Science."

"What do you mean?"

"Well, let's for the moment assume that we really are all One, and even more, that All is One. If this were true, then there would be only one thing in the universe, in fact the universe would be that one thing. Also, there would be no such thing as time and no such thing as space. Everything would be happening *here, now*!

"So in such a case, it wasn't Ron who phoned me; it was myself doing so. Similarly, it wasn't you interrupting me, but myself. I did these things (or rather I am in the process of doing them now) because I needed to do them in

One

order to develop in the way that I had visualized. Or rather, doing them and developing and visualizing are happening at the same time, now, and so they are all the same action."

"But I was conscious of interrupting you," Mary spoke, a bit puzzled. "And Ron was likely aware of phoning you. Are you saying that he and I don't exist?"

"No, of course you exist. But you and Ron are the same as me. We are all One. And yet, you both acted independently from me, as you said. So I'll bet that Ron needed to grow or develop in some way that was best done by phoning me. Also you needed to develop in some way that was best enabled by interrupting me and thus having this conversation. I don't know what the result will be for either of you."

"So we all exist as separate people, but at the same time we are all One?" asked Mary.

"Yeah! Hard to understand, huh? But it explains so much."

"So, does this mean that I'm a slave to you, to do whatever you need for your development?"

"Wow, you ask good questions, Mary! No, certainly not. Nobody is a slave to anyone else. We all have the ability to decide on things for ourselves. Yes, it is true that I needed someone, indeed, I *created* someone or some situation, to do some action that would help my development. But it wasn't me that sent you the intuitive urge to do the action that was needed. It was God, or the universal creative intelligence, that did so. If it was up to me to decide who should act on my behalf, I would almost certainly foul it up by picking the wrong person or urging the wrong action. But God sees a far bigger picture than I do, and can chose just the right person, and give just the right urging, to make the most effective impact on me, and at the same time make the most effective impact on that other person."

"That sure is a different view of God than we learned in Sunday School! How do you know all these things?" Mary was totally engrossed in the conversation, fascinated by what she was hearing, but partly incredulous that her own sister could have such far-out ideas.

Jane thought for a moment, soberly. What if she were wrong? What is she were misleading a young, impressionable mind, that of her own sister? How could she be so presumptuous as to think that she had all the answers?

One

Then she glanced at the poster on her wall with another of her favourite quotes:

> *I don't have all the answers,*
> *but I know Someone who does!*

That gave her courage, because she was certain that through her prayer and meditation she was getting the answers from the proper Someone.

"Yes, you're right. My view of God certainly has changed! I have to be careful not to impose my views on you, Mary. I've developed a view of reality that seems to work for me, but I can't honestly say for certain that it is the completely correct view. And I'm also sure that my conception of God will continue to evolve.

"And I'm not sure that my current views contradict the old Sunday School stories of God. I think that they are the same, but I see them now with a broader and more general interpretation.

"And as for how I know all these things .... Well, I can't say that I *know* them. But I believe them. I sort of use them like a Science experiment, testing them in various situations to see if they fit with reality. And, like I said, they seem to work for me at this point in my life."

The girls paused and sat silently for a few moments.

Mary spoke first. "You sound as wise as an old person, like, as if you were twenty years old."

"Ho! That's a good one, Little Sister! I can't imagine being twenty. That would be like, over the hill! And yet, there's so much to learn, and to contribute. I'll need twenty times twenty years!"

"And you'll get them, won't you, if what they say about reincarnation is true."

"Yes. And if you want spooky, listen to this!"

Mary leaned forward, ready, wide-eyed.

"I don't think I've ever told you," continued Jane, "that I remember before I was born, seeing this body, this family, this life, and being sucked down into Mom's newborn baby as it took its first breath."

One

"Holy, flippin' molasses!" exclaimed Mary. "Were you in heaven, and came back?"

"Well ... the simple answer is Yes. The longer answer would take a while—let's just say that I was living in a very beautiful place where I was learning about the lessons of previous lives, and I was preparing for this life."

"So, did you see Mom and Dad ... you know ... doing it, to make you?"

"No," replied Jane. "I don't remember that, but I'm quite certain that I could have seen it if I had wanted to do so. I forget most of what I was aware of before coming into this body, sort of like you forget dreams, but a distinct memory that I have is that I saw the reason for my birth."

"So tell me!"

"I have a vivid memory, all in a single flash, of seeing the whole world in a state of decay, like it was losing its life. I could see that Mom would do something that would save it, and that I would help her somehow."

"Wow! The L-movement!"

Why Are Gas Prices So High?

"Yeah, I guess so. For sure, Mom made a great contribution, but I'm not sure what I did to help."

"Well, you did your school report, and you rooted for Mom. And besides, maybe your big thing is yet to come. Or maybe you heard God telling you what to say."

"Yeah. Thanks."

Another pause, to think over the enormity of the topic that they were discussing.

Jane looked very pensive. "You know, I was just thinking. You're right! This idea of creating the future through visualization ... that's what God does, too. Holy cow! Can you imagine it? It's so boggling! As above, so below! Like Joe said ...."

"What do you mean?" asked Mary, sensing her sister's excitement.

"Oh! It's amazing! Let's see if I can explain. So, can you see what I meant about causing Ron and you to act, by visualizing myself as highly effective. Can you accept that, Mary?"

"OK, I believe you."

One

"Well, God did the same thing with me. Oh! I feel like crying, it's so beautiful!"

Mary moved over to hug Jane. "Tell me about it."

Tears moistened Jane's eyes, as she struggled to explain. "Well, in just the same way that I needed someone else to do something to give me a nudge in the right direction—in this case I needed someone to interrupt me to remind me of my role in others' lives—in just the same way, God needed someone to act here on earth to give Mom a nudge in the right direction to achieve the future that she would be creating through her own visualizing.

"So God sent me!

"And I now realize that it explains the dream I had this morning, just as I was waking up. In my dream Mom thanked me for telling her to slow down, because that inspired her to think of slowing down to drive the speed limit.

"Isn't that a boggling bunch of things to think about?" Jane almost collapsed with the relief of seeing such a big picture and understanding it.

"And you came through again, Little Sister! Oh! I could hug you to pieces!" Jane lunged at her and wrapped her arms around her.

"Hey, what did I do?" asked Mary.

"You suggested that maybe God had told me what to say, and that opened up an area of my memory to realize that you were right."

"Wow! Boggling is right!" breathed Mary.

"Yeah! It sure is!" Jane observed.

"You know," she continued, "What it feels like is being evolved further than many others. I don't mean better, but simply more evolved.

"You see, evolution continues. It didn't stop when fish developed legs or people learned to walk upright. Humans are still evolving, and we have so very far to go, not just with physical development, but more importantly with psychic development. That's what we're talking about here."

She paused, breathed deeply, and gazed inward. She saw far inside—and vastly far outside, glimpsing a cosmic reality that was even more vast, but more harmonious, than she could have asked for or imagined. She felt profoundly peaceful, with tears of joy.

"And yet," Jane continued, "We are all One. All other families are our family. There by the Grace of God go I. All the earth and all its people are us. The L-movement is a natural reaction to society's reckless action of abandoning the Oneness of All. And it wasn't Mom or me who started that reaction. It was everyone acting together, all as One, following intuitive urges."

Part D: The Present Time

CHAPTER 14 *A new world*

Tuxedos and formal black gowns.

That was the dress code for the ceremony at Rideau Hall, the official residence of Canada's Governor General.

The girls could hardly believe it! Their mother was going to be awarded the Order of Canada! And they and their father were invited to be in the audience.

The Order of Canada recognizes people who have made a significant contribution to the country. It is Canada's highest honour for lifetime achievement. Twice

165

per year, the Governor General awards more than 100 such honours to distinguished Canadians.

- - -

Claire Robertson Atwater.

The uniformed, ceremonial soldier of the Governor General's Foot Guards accompanied Claire from the back of the room, along the centre aisle, through the applauding crowd of guests, and right up to the point where she stood in front of the Governor General and her husband.

Jane, Mary, and Peter had the loudest applause, biggest smiles, and moistest eyes.

The announcer read out the citation for Claire's award:

> *Having popularized the notion of driving the speed limit in order to save on gas consumption, Claire Atwater has been credited with the founding of the popular "L-movement." The movement was spontaneously adopted world-wide, and has had profound and lasting effects on global ecological sustainability and on personal well-being. The awesome power of a single person's idea, applied at the right time, has been demonstrated through this movement, and it serves as an inspiration to all.*

A new world

Claire wished that her family could be standing here, sharing the spotlight with her. And Joe. And all the other people who had encouraged her and followed her suggestion. Her family, Joe, all those others—they were the real heroes, not her. She had merely suggested driving the speed limit. They had adopted her advice and put it into action. They were the ones who had saved the world.

Suddenly she realized in a flash that it was Jane who had inspired her, by singing "Slow down and live" that morning, three years ago. Claire turned around, looked straight at Jane in the audience, and mouthed the words, "Thank you!" to her. Immediately, Jane realized that this was exactly what she had dreamed about, nearly a year ago. Through her tears, she smiled, nodded, and mouthed back to her mother, "I know! You're welcome!" The dream had shown her the future, which was in reality—and which now had become—the present.

So God needed me to prompt Mom! thought Jane. *He probably also guided Joe to ask his famous question at that famous lunch. What else? Mary? Dad? Maybe even gas prices had to go up—God forced them up—so that our family would come to be—and the L-movement starts—and humanity gets saved and the world gets saved! This is all so very amazing ... The Oneness of it All! I think I'm going to wet my pants!*

When will he stop? wondered Claire. *Where should I look? All those people looking at me, smiling. Smile back. No! Look sober, distinguished, humble ... controlled, calm, happy ... proud, grateful.*

Claire Robertson Atwater.

Ah! It's over!

Applause. The Governor General stood up, smiled graciously as she pinned the medal onto Claire's lapel, embraced her, kissed both cheeks, and said a few personal words of sincere congratulations. Then the Governor General's husband shook Claire's hand and offered his congratulations also. Claire had to be told afterwards what had happened, for she was hardly conscious of where she was.

Then she was escorted off to the side, as the applause was subsiding, to sign the register, and then to join the other new members of the Order of Canada.

- - -

A new world

"Did you hear the news about air pollution?" Jane was excited to tell her parents.

They were relaxing in their Ottawa hotel rooms, the day after the Order of Canada ceremony had occurred. The reception, banquet, and speeches were a mellow glow in yesterday's memories. Today they had taken a tour of Ottawa, went to an official lunch, and did some shopping. Now they were watching television, taking a break before going out that evening to dinner and a concert at the National Arts Centre.

Jane had burst into her parents' room from the adjoining room where the girls were staying. "Quick, turn to channel 7!"

Peter jumped when his daughter said 'Jump' in that tone of voice, and had the TV switched to channel 7 in a heartbeat. They caught the end of the news item ...

> ... *So it would seem that the movement to drive the speed limit has truly had an effect on the earth's atmosphere. As Dr. Stevens mentioned, the data are preliminary and need to be confirmed by other labs, but his group is the first to announce some actual measurements of a slight turnaround, after some forty years of air pollution buildup. If this good*

169

news turns out to be true, then it will provide a stunning vindication for the originators and proponents of the L-movement.

For his views, we welcome once again our Science commentator, Jason Matthews.

"Wow! This is fantastic! Way to go, Mom!" Jane and Mary could barely contain their excitement.

... Yes, I agree, John. This is good news. And my guess is that the data will be confirmed by others. Dr. Stevens has a reputation of being very conservative and cautious. He would not release this report prematurely, just to grab the limelight. No—I think that this result is just the start of lots of reports about measured improvements in greenhouse gas reductions and less air pollution, not just predictions or speculations, but hard data on the earth bouncing back.

"Yahoo!" they all cheered.

But, do you know what is even better? Any day now we will hear an announcement by some social researcher that even more impressive results are now being measured in a lowering of peoples' stress levels, greater social civility, and lessening health care costs. I know this, because I have been

A new world

privy to one or two draft papers on the subject, but it would be wrong of me to reveal any details yet.

"Oh! This is wonderful!" thought Claire, choking back tears.

What great timing this is, receiving this report about improving air quality! Just yesterday Claire Atwater was made a Member of the Order of Canada for having started the L-movement, which is credited with a direct cause of these improvements.

I sure hope that Claire and her family are watching this program now!

Printed in the United States
54819LVS00001B/73-75